Room Tone

Room Tone

a novella by

Gale Zoë Garnett

QUATTRO BOOKS

This is a work of fiction. Names, characters, places and incidents are either
the product of the author's imagination or are used fictitiously, and any resem-
blance to actual persons, living or dead, business establishments, events or
locales is entirely coincidental.

Cover Design and Typography: Julie McNeill, McNeill Design Arts

Author Photo: Cylla von Tiedemann

Library and Archives Canada Cataloguing in Publication

Garnett, Gale Zoë
Room tone : a novella / by Gale Zoë Garnett.

ISBN 978-0-9782806-1-1

I. Title.

PS8563.A6732R66 2007   C813'.54   C2007-900590-X

Published by
Quattro Books
P.O. Box 53031
Royal Orchard Postal Station
10 Royal Orchard Blvd.
Thornhill, ON L3T 3C0
www.quattrobooks.ca

Printed in Canada

For Walter Lassally
&
Tom Shoebridge

Étonne moi! (Astonish me!)

— Jean Cocteau to his film actors

1 Vedettine in Paris

I FELL IN LOVE WITH FILM because my mother was sleeping with the ugliest man in Paris. I didn't call him that. I was ten and had certainly not seen all the men in Paris. "The Ugliest Man in Paris" was simply part of his name — Jean Marie Carignac, the Ugliest Man in Paris.

Most Parisians actually liked the way Carignac looked. Particularly the youngest ones. Children were noticeably happy to see him. How could we not be? A small bandy-legged pipe-smoking bearded man who wore an apple green slightly pointy wool cap over his midnight black shoulder-length hair. His face was creased with folded lines like a Shar-Pei dog but they opened like accordion pleats when he smiled. He had a hugely wide grin and tiny teeth, stained yellow from years of smoking unfiltered Gauloises Bleu. His trousers were either chocolate-brown or forest-green wide-wale corduroy and his silky white or butter-yellow shirts were blouse-y and piratical. His shiny, bunched-up black leather boots added to the Short John Silver effect. Children want proof that fairy tales are real. Jean Marie Carignac was proof.

His voice was low and rumbly, so it frequently sounded as if he were saying *aarrggh!* More accurately *bohnbahngrahhng* — the French equivalent of *aarrggh!*

What child would not love such a person? This one certainly did. And always will.

Carignac presided over wide-ranging discussions at a large round table in *Le Cochon qui Danse*, a Montmartre bistrot. He would hold forth on all things cinematic and some things political, surrounded by acolytes of all ages, many of whom called him "Maître" with the familiar warmth one would use to say "Mon ami."

He had directed only one major film, *Le Boulot de Ma Mère* (My Mother's Job), about a little boy whose mother killed people for the Marseilles mob. The film was considered a "classic" and many world art-film people took him up as a hero. He then founded *La Cinémathèque de Montmartre* and discovered his passionate commitment to teaching. People came from throughout France and, eventually, the world, to study with him. Even those who were already celebrated became students of *Carignac, Le Maître*, who very occasionally would still co-direct films made by one or another of his young protégés, sometimes even playing small acting roles. "It is necessary to keep the practical experience if one is to grow as a teacher," he explained.

When these Bistrot discussions happened on a Friday night, Maman would sometimes take me with her. The Carignac Gang would greet me, the little daughter of Laure Normand and Bo Lindskog, with hugs, kisses and chin-chucks. After which I would sit silently, listening, looking at the faces, some of which were very well-known.

My favourite face (and body) belonged to Tilly Duber, the great German character actress, who had lived in Paris and worked in French films and plays since fleeing Hitler in 1933.

Tilly's lemon yellow and bright orange Toulouse-Lautrec hair was knotted up at the top of her head like a hairy peach. The place her lips had once more fully filled was outlined in raspberry pencil and coloured in with an impasto of fuchsia lipstick. Pale parchment-thin skin was cross-hatched with lines. Out of this ancient visage peered the huge round brown eyes of a curious child. Her voice was clear and strong, but when she laughed her throat would fill with nicotine-fuelled phlegm, which she cleared with one room-rocking cough. As with Carignac, Tilly had a *costume personnel*: black tights, ballooning black skirt covering her ballooning bum. Breasts the shape and almost the size of two hippopotamus snouts rested under an old shapeless and nubbly-covered magenta cashmere sweater. A large black cardigan that had probably once belonged to a man (Maman said that Tilly had been the long-time lover — "a thousand years ago" — of Freddy Hirsch, a brilliant director whose Hitler-flight took him to America and three American film Oscars) completed the ensemble.

Tilly smoked using a long onyx and ivory cigarette holder. Her shoes were always the same. Pointy, black and laced up to mid-calf. She was about the same tiny height as Carignac. As they often walked about Paris together, they were sometimes, with affection, called "The Witch and the Gnome."

At *Le Cochon qui Danse*, Maman would sit almost as silent as I, inhaling every word Carignac uttered, only speaking in support of his arguments.

My sex-to-cinema connection was this: Carignac's Cinémathèque had become the most important film school in Europe. Many of its directors and actors (including my mother) had gone on to national and international success.

The Cinémathèque had a full schedule of courses and master classes — cinématography, acting-for-camera, set design, directing, art directing, screenwriting, costume design, light and sound technologies. It also contained the best cinéma in Paris.

Sound was what got me sent to the cinéma.

Feeling fluey, eyes and nose running, I'd been excused from school two hours early, so that I would not, in the ever doom-laden words of my teacher, Madame Grenier, "poison the other students."

I arrived at our Montparnasse apartment and heard my mother being murdered (or, as Mme. Grenier would say, *ah-sasseeNAY!*).

Reflexively, I rushed to save my screaming mum. Grabbing the cold belly of one of our brass dolphin doorpulls, I flung open the carved oak doors of the master bedroom and was staring at Jean Marie Carignac's round fuzzy buttocks. He was sort of climbing my mother, who was tall for a French woman. Over his shoulder, Maman regarded me with alarm, her eyes and mouth in the shape of an O. "Good day, my little Dominique," she said. "You have returned to the house early from the Lycée."

What I had seen was not referred to at our *coq au vin* dinner, out of sensitivity for the feelings of my father. My parents had what would come to be called "an open marriage." They each, with public discretion and personal courtesy, had other relationships — Maman more than Papa (My father loved making films; my mother loved being desired. They both loved me).

As Carignac was called "The Ugliest Man in Paris," my father, Bo Lindskog, was called "The Best Cinematographer in Europe." I frequently wondered if, in the French fashion, I would have a title when I grew up. I hoped I might inherit my mother's title: "One of the Most Beautiful Women in Paris." A few days later, being half-Swedish (and not as good-looking as Maman), I amended this to "Most Attractive."

Maman's *coq au vin* was a good dish and frequently served. She said that her *répertoire de la cuisine* was smaller than her versatility as an actress, but that she hoped we were always pleased by what she prepared. We assured her that we were. Always. And I thought (but did not say) that *anything* she made was better than my father's *Lutefisk*, a Swedish Christmas fish dish that was rather nasty even when exquisitely prepared.

I sipped the family cold-and-flu medication-watered Gevry Chambertin mixed with the juice of half a lemon — as we discussed versatility and coq. During dessert, Maman produced a shiny apple-green laminated card.

"*Eh voila, Dominique!*" she cried happily, presenting me with the card, saying I was now the youngest member of the Cinémathèque de Montmartre, and could, for no money at all, go to films at the Cinémathèque's Cinéma whenever I was not in school, or at dinner or in bed.

Later, when Papa was in the study reading his Swedish newspaper, Maman told me that I could go to the Cinémathèque any time I was free, but, most particularly, I should go between the hours of two and six in the afternoon. Even at ten I understood the implications of her instruction. To this day I do not think of Carignac without imagining his buoyant fuzzy bum bouncing atop my mother while a bright sliver of sun-light streamed through the parting in the floor-length floral curtains.

Papa was as tall as Carignac was small. Papa's mother, Farmor Lindskog, was also tall. Many Swedes are tall, especially to a child. As a small child, I would walk up to tall blonde people in Paris and ask if they were Swedish. If they were, they smiled and said I was smart and pretty. If they were Norwegian, they corrected my mistake. If they were Danish, they corrected me more gently but said they were "indeed Nordic." Parisians tilted their heads, raised an eyebrow and proudly proclaimed themselves Parisians — and one elderly Frenchwoman from the 16th Arrondissement said I was very rude to ask such questions of someone unknown to me and that her ancestors were not my affair.

1974's *Cinéma da la Cinémathèque de Montmartre* was a revelation. I had already seen many films — mostly those of my parents (unless they were deemed too scary or violent; this applied particularly to the noir-style detective films in which Maman co-starred with the Greek-American expatriate actor, Stav Karras). None of this prepared me for the enormous basket of film on show at the Cinémathèque — films from everywhere in the world and in all sorts of languages (with sub-titles).

Most amazing of all: the Cinéma would run films for 20 hours per day, even on Sundays. Cinémathèque members could see *Casablanca* at three in the Morning, *Les Diaboliques* (with its knifed eyeball) just after breakfast, and *The Seventh Seal* at Midnight. There were always at least three or four people watching whatever film was screening.

Sometimes I would recognise a face in the audience. If the face belonged to someone who'd been to our apartment, we would wave or nod briefly, two cinéastes come to silently worship at the temple (one of the worshippers being a ten-year-old girl).

During screenings, we cinéastes made a barely perceptible collective sound. The sound of people in a room, breathing together, safe inside a cloak of both darkness and magical flickering light: an enormous palette made entirely of the colour range between deepest black and brightest white. This light would play on our faces but we did not usually see one another's faces because we were all looking at the huge wondrous faces on the screen.

Alone and together. For a child, afraid, as all children are afraid (whether they admit it or not) of both alone and together, combining them was a perfect solution. Combining two fearful things equalled no fear. Mme. Krassowicz, who taught Latin at the Lycée, said that combining two bad things to produce a good thing was called a "litote." The Cinéma was my litote.

Maman had said I should go to the Cinéma in the afternoon. On my first afternoon I stayed from three to seven, seeing a short film about voodoo (Vodoun) in Haiti, *Le Ballon Rouge,* and *The Wizard of Oz* before rushing home on the Metro and being fifteen minutes late for dinner.

I was so excited by what I'd seen: "… and the Haitian people go into a dancing trance … then all the balloons in Paris come from everywhere and lift the little boy, Pascal, into the sky … and Dorothy clicks her sparkly red shoes three times and she and her little dog are blown into this extraordinary place!"

My parents forgave my tardiness, obviously delighted that I'd been thunderstruck by the Family Business.

They had no idea just *how* thunderstruck. Occasionally, I would forge my mother's loopy theatrical signature under typed notes excusing me from classes at the Lycée. On the days preceding these bogus notes, I would stay all day at the Cinéma, seeing three or four films before going home.

The best cinémadventure was waiting for my parents to be asleep and then getting the last train to Montmartre before the Metro closed at midnight. Gérard, the projectionist, was surprised to see me at so late an hour, but I assured him that I had permission to see midnight films "from time to time." A long-time family friend, Gérard looked a bit suspicious and said he would drive me home after the screenings. Having never been out on my own after midnight, I was glad of this, though I did assure Gérard that I had taxi-money from my allowance savings.

Tip-toeing back into our apartment, I collided with my father, who was off to shoot a film (film set-ups tended to begin before dawn). In a nervous speedy whisper, I told him where I'd been and what I'd seen (*The Third Man*, *Showboat*, and *The Four Horsemen of the Apocalypse* — with live piano music!).

Trying to look stern, Papa said, "Écoute, Dominique ... it is wonderful that you are so engaged with film, but you must get your rest and you must go to school. So, if you wish to attend the Cinéma on your own in the middle of the night, you may only do this once a month, on a Friday or Saturday. And only if Gérard or I myself can bring you home. I will organise this with Gérard."

My Cinéma attendance soon fused with my dreams. While I slept, men ran through watery sewers or, in sparkly red shoes, I stood with Rudolph Valentino in the middle of a brightly coloured field, into which I'd been gently parachuted by bouquets of balloons.

Before long I had yet another secret — one unknown to even my conspiratorial father: I was in love.

My beloved's name was Nikolai Tcherkhassov. He was the star of a Russian film called *Alexandre Nevsky*. Having only just passed my tenth birthday, I did not understand much of *Alexandre Nevsky*. I did understand the big face and muscular body of Nikolai Tcherkhassov. I'd had momentarily urgent crushes on teenaged boys as well as intermittent fantasies about Pierre Dufresne, a French film star who'd acted with my mother in two films, and who visited our apartment from time to time with his housemate, costume designer Ludovico Celli. Maman said, "Pierre and Ludovico are a loving couple, for many years, like Claude LaBrecque and Hubert Lemelin" (two other family friends). M. Dufresne had been married once, so his romantic contentment with M. Celli did not prevent my writing "Mme. Dominique Dufresne" ten times on a page of my school notebook, then tearing out the page, afraid of being teased by anyone who might see it.

I was already being teased because my speaking voice was so low, and had been since I was six. A small cluster of Lycée girls, led by Clothilde Lussier, the prettiest girl in drama class, would sometimes follow me to the Metro making deep bass "wo-wo-wo" noises. Clothilde also called me "Vedettine" (because my mother was famous). Or, because of my low voice, "Vedettine the Frog." This title reminded me of "Carignac, the Ugliest Man in Paris." I did not want "Vedettine the Frog" to become my title. I felt fairly certain it would not, as long as it could be kept at school, remaining unknown to the general population of Paris.

Clothilde stopped calling me "Vedettine" after she actually *met* Maman, who fetched me from school one day, in order to take me for a haircut. She was dazzled by Maman. Maman told her that she was gracious and charming, so she decided to become gracious and charming, in the hope that Maman would invite her to dine with us. She thought dining with us would help her to become a film star, which was what she planned to do while waiting to marry a rich man with a title (not a title like "The Ugliest Man in Paris;" a title like "Duc" or "Baron").

After meeting Clothilde, Maman said, "You see, my little Dominique — if you give people a part of what they want they will treat you well because they want the rest of it. Your little tormentor wants to be a film star. It will never happen with that name. *Clothilde!* Only good for a baker with enormous flapping flesh-flag arms and fat fingers!"

At that point, I did not care so much about Clothilde. I cared, cared every day, about my Great Love, M. Nikolai Tcherkhassov. Big face, silky pale hair, large powerful hands to hold and caress me. Just thinking these things would make it hard to breathe normally. My breath would block at the back of my throat and, if I were alone, I would cup my hands over my tiny breasts and squeeze. The squeezing would break the blockage and I'd exhale.

Mon Nikolai — N.T., as I would, more discreetly, write in my notebook, became my first Pillow Lover. At night, in my bed and under the duvet, I would hug and kiss my pillow, calling it by his name. "Ohhh, Nikolai! Yes, Nikolai! Hold me, mon Nikolai, until I fall asleep. I love you too."

After meeting Maman, Clothilde was quite friendly to me, inviting me to go to the Patisserie with her cotérie after school. I thanked her but said I could not, that I was rushing off to meet "a special friend." I would not say who.

My special friend was, of course, Nikolai Tcherkhassov and the film was *Peter the Great*.

When *Peter the Great* ended, the Art Deco wall-sconce lights of the Cinéma came up. In the small-windowed room above my head, a man unspooled one film and threaded up the next.

I decided to walk the long distance from Montmartre to Montparnasse so that Mon Nikolai and I could walk together, holding hands and talking softly about our lives. If anyone noted the tallish girl with smallish breasts who was talking to herself and swinging her lightly-fisted hand back and forth while ambling home, I was unaware of it.

The following day, during lunch, Clothilde pressed me for the name of my *ami special*. I blushed, giggled and finally said he was called Nikolai Tcherkhassov and that he was a Russian film star and a friend of my family. I said that Nikolai and I had met in the previous year when he came to dinner at our apartment.

The following day Clothilde and her cotérie were waiting for me in front of the Lycée. They were laughing and shouting, *"Liar, Liar! Voix de grenouille!* Vedettine is a frog-voiced liar. Wo-wo-wo!"

Flushed and frightened, I moved past them quickly. Schoolmates were looking at us, and feeling some safety in numbers, I turned to face my tormentors.

"Clothilde! Anne-Marie, Marguerite! What is this about?"

Clothilde moved forward, stabbing the air with her index finger and jutting out her chin and lower lip.

"Nikolai Tcherkhassov? Your special friend? He died when you were two years old! He was sixty-six when he died! An old man! My mother is half-Russian. She knows these films. She loved your special friend when she was your age. She did not know him either; she loved him in the Cinéma. Just like you, Vedettine! Only *you're* in love with a dead man! A dead old man!"

It seems such a small moment now, but I can still feel it, remember the talc, metal and disinfectant smell of the Lycée corridor, the blush-flush heat of my cheeks, the feeling dizzy but refusing to faint.

That night, as we ate our *coq au vin*, I told my parents what I'd done and what had resulted. Water came out of my eyes but I made no crying noises (my mother hated crying noises and my father was slightly embarrassed by them). Papa rubbed the back of my hand, then squeezed it. His eyes, always sea-under-ice sparkly, like dolls' eyes, were soft. I spoke to what I saw there.

"Yes Papa, your daughter is an embarrassment. An idiot and a liar. A liar who got caught."

"Nonono, Dominique," Maman said indignantly, though her eyes were twinkling and I was afraid she would laugh. "You are not an idiot. All young girls have secret love with film stars. And frequently say they know them. I felt this love for Gérard Philipe, after seeing *Le Rouge et le noir* at a small cinéma in the 5th Arrondissement. I told no one. Monsieur Philipe had died when I was a small girl. I knew this. In the future, my little Dominique, it would probably be best for you to know if the man you love is still alive."

In bed later that night, I felt scraped raw, pulpy. Outside the window, a slightly nibbled full moon shone.

Papa knocked at my door, asking if he could enter. "Oui, Papa, entré," I said softly. He sat on the edge of my bed, brushing hair out of my eyes, then resting his long-fingered hand against my cheek. "How is it with you, my Nica? Any better?" he asked. I did not have the language to say how it was with me — at least not language that did not include the word shit. I shook my head.

"Listen, Nica. Tomorrow, I want you to stay home from school and come with me to the Cinémathèque."

The Cinémathèque! Cause of my broken heart. Cause of my humiliation. I emphatically shook my head, saying "No, Papa. No

Cinémathèque. Not for a while. I do not want to see ... Monsieur Tcherkhassov for a while. I do not ..."

"This is not about him, Nica. It's about you. There is someone I want you to meet."

The film was called *Shanghai Express*. Its star, Marlene Dietrich, had fine blonde hair, as did my father and I. Maman was also blonde, though her blondeness was courtesy of a woman called Rosie Carita, who coloured the hair of most of the women, and some of the men, in French cinéma.

I knew at once that I would never be as beautiful as Mlle. Dietrich, but that wasn't the important part. The important part, the part my father wanted me to know, was her voice. It was so low. So "wo-wo-wo." So "Vedettine the Frog." So very beautiful.

Papa saw me see it. Saw me hear it. Saw me understand it. Out of the corner of my eye I could see him smiling. "Exakt, Nica. Preciss," he whispered in Swedish.

We walked home, me holding the real hand of my father, as I'd once held the fantasy hand of Nikolai Tcherkhassov. There was so much love in it. Not romantic love. Something deeper. Something filled with hope. A love that believed what Papa said as we crossed the Boulevard Montparnasse — all would be well once my face and body caught up with my voice.

After hot chocolate with Papa, as I headed down the hall to wash and go to bed, I turned and, lowering then raising my eyes as Miss Dietrich had done, dropped my voice to its most basso place and repeated the best line from *Shanghai Express*.

"It took more than one man to name me Shanghai Lily."

"Indeed, Nica, indeed!" Papa replied, and we both laughed.

I made it a point to see other early Marlene Dietrich films at the Cinémathèque — *Morocco, Blonde Venus,* and *The Blue Angel*. After Papa and I saw this last film (his favourite), he taught me to sing "Falling in Love Again," in German and English. Sometimes I would sing this when we had guests. The guests, usually film people, were clearly delighted, particularly liking my "throaty" voice. "Throaty," I thought. "My voice is *not* frog-like. It is throaty."

And Mlle. Dietrich had wonderful cheekbones. My mother had wonderful cheekbones. I pressed at my round child-cheeks, certain I could feel the bones under them, bones waiting to be born in the better life that was coming.

Six months after seeing my future at the Cinéma, I awakened with my bed, nightdress and legs covered in blood. The blood was coming from somewhere in my vagina. I screamed. Maman was away filming, so my poor father rushed to my room and tried to explain. It seemed he could either look at me or explain, so I told him to look at the wall and to please tell me if I was bleeding to death. Eyes fixed on a watercolour of the Rue Galande, he assured me that all of this was normal and that it would bring me the body that went with my voice.

"Big breasts?" I enquired eagerly.

"Probably not enormous. Your mother's breasts are … not enormous. But sufficient, I am sure."

Still staring at the watercolour, he told me the bleeding would be a monthly occurrence, except during pregnancy, and that it got rid of bad blood and kept good blood, and that I needed to take a shower and to then insert a tampon.

"In the hole?"

"Yes. In the hole."

"Will I still be able to make peepee?"

"Yes. Yes you will. Now, go and shower, Nica, and I will change your bedsheets."

Poor Papa. It was, I could see, a very difficult sort of information for a man to have to present to his daughter.

When I returned from the shower, he gave me a handful of tampons for my book bag, saying that I should replace a tampon with a fresh one three or four times a day, and that he would buy me a few boxes while I was at school.

"A few boxes?! How long does this bleeding go on, Papa?"

"Not so long. Usually, I think, about five days. It only happens to women, but I think four or five days is correct."

"It, the tampon, is … very fat."

"Your mother uses 'super'. I will get you 'regular'."

"Am I not … not super?"

He nodded vigorously. "Oh yes, Nica, you are super. You are *superbe* … but, for beginning all this, regular will be more … comfortable."

En route to the Lycée, feeling like I'd been stuffed with a huge cotton egg, I thought about The Hole.

Girls at school would sometimes discuss The Hole. Clothilde said babies came out of The Hole. I thought she was just saying this to frighten me — when she described all these horrors I pretended to have known all this forever. But I'd seen babies and I'd seen The Hole, and it didn't seem possible that something as big as a baby could possibly come out of something as small as The Hole. That night I asked Maman. She assured me that babies did this, and said I had come out of her Hole (she put this in more genteel language but the information completely supported Clothilde's theory of Babies and Holes).

Naturally, I then asked Maman who put the babies in the holes in the first place. Her answer confirmed an even more terrifying Lycée gigglesecret.

At that point in my life, I'd seen only two penises (three, if you counted the one in the Spanish film). One was my father's — twice — in the shower and at a nude beach in the South of France. The other was a purplish limp thing that had fallen out of the open-flied trousers of a drunken old man asleep in front of a café. These penises, even my father's, which was twice the size of the small snaky blob of the drunken man, were considerably smaller than babies were. Yet, because they went *in* instead of coming *out,* incoming penises seemed scarier than outgoing babies. I decided not to think about it until I had to.

And then the bleeding happened. And the tampon. If the tampon felt so uncomfortable, penises and babies were going to be completely hell.

When Maman returned from filming, she apologised profusely for not having got the bleeding information to me in time. Her own first blood had come when she was eleven-and-a-half years old. Seeing most things in relation to herself, Maman thought she had about a year before worrying me unnecessarily by having to discuss something "so messy and annoying."

For all my new blood-borne messy annoyance, I still hoped it would, like my voice, work better once I was a bit older. My father had said it would. My father is a very wise man. And he was right.

The bleeding was the beginning of about seven years of changes, some in me, others in the people and circumstances that surrounded me.

The best of the first changes involved Clothilde Lussier — more accurately, it *uninvolved* her — in my life.

Clothilde's father had inherited the family home and business in Lyon, and the Lussiers went off to live there. Without a ringleader, Clothilde's cotérie lost interest in tormenting me. It was also true that they too were having body-changes and had turned inward to monitor themselves, not to mention their outward turn that involved clothing, subtle enhancements, and boys.

Also very happily true was that, taller, apparently prettier and with a newly curvaceous though still thin body (and newly prominent cheekbones), "Vedettine" became the vedette of the Lycée Drama Society. Between the ages of ten and 13, I starred in six school productions, including *Romeo and Juliet, Dear Brutus, This Property Is Condemned, The Playboy of the Western World, The Bald Soprano,* and *Ondine.*

My résumé continued to grow at my next school, École de Mougins, a private school in Provence. While there I also got a small role in a film shooting nearby in Cannes. Maman said I was "so beautiful. The camera loves you." Papa said, "Good, Nica. You now have a small piece of film to show people who want to see how you photograph. You must learn to blink less; you have lovely eyes and the camera wants to see them not jumping so much."

By the time I was graduated from École de Mougins it was clear that I was going into the Family Business.

Also clear was that my parents' Open Marriage had opened so wide it would no longer close. Maman fell for Mario Zavani, a young Italian film star — "I am madly in love, an amour fou, my little Dominique!" she wrote me at school. Papa, who was sure this coup de foudre would be short-lived, also, with no malice ("more a desire for peace and quiet, a desire to simplify my life, a desire to return to Stockholm") agreed to an amicable divorce. Maman and Mario lasted almost a year. To be followed by Maman and Jorge, Maman and Nigel, Maman and Olivier (a two-year marriage), and Maman and Gaspard ("I hate his name," she explained, "but love his smell").

When I finished, with honours, at École de Mougins, the family had a career-conference.

It was agreed that while my Swedish was acceptable, my two fluent languages were French and, thanks to school, English.

It was agreed that acting studies in English would open my career to greater international possibilities.

It was agreed that I would change my name to Nica Lind. Maman said, "Nobody outside of the Nordic World will like the 'Skog'. Too harsh. And your father has always called you 'Nica'. It already belongs to you."

It was agreed that I would apply to English theatre and film schools, and, as a member of La Cinémathèque de Montmartre, I could also take courses there whenever I was in Paris.

It was agreed that I would keep my usual room in our Montparnasse apartment and also a small room with a fine view in my father's Gamla Stan flat in Stockholm (which he'd inherited years earlier and had let to friends, who would now be given time to move).

It was agreed that my life as a professional actress was about to begin.

2 Nica Lind Enters the Family Business

PAPA SAYS IT IS IMPORTANT to know what makes you happy. If you know the things that make you happy, you will, even when you cannot have those things, know where to point yourself; when to open out and say, "It's me. I'm here. I'm here to give and to receive and to make use of the things that make me happy."

Acting, from the first moment I did it at school, made me happy. Happy and safe, nested inside the paradox of a controlled world where I could be completely free.

Sometimes the situation of the person I was playing tore my guts up, but even then, under that bleeding, crying, aching place I was happy, because the core seed, the *noyau* of me, knew I was doing what I was meant to do.

At seventeen, I applied to the six most esteemed acting schools in the UK. Due, I imagine, to my parents' professional achievements, I was asked to interview and audition at all six. Five accepted me.

I decided on The London Academy of Theatre and Film for three reasons.

1. They gave equal weight to cinéma (British schools tend to privilege theatre over all other forms of acting; LATF did not).
2. It was an intensive one-year course, rather than the university model, which took years.
3. Jamie Concannon.

At my first audition and interview with him, I chose Jamie Concannon, LATF's Artistic Director, as the man who would be my first lover. Fortunately, he chose me in return, though not until the middle of my student year.

I was most definitely not his first lover. Nor did I wish to be. When I was sixteen, Maman, after asking if I was *encore vierge,* advised me quite emphatically not to start with an inexperienced person ("If you, neither one nor the other, knows anything, it will be clumsy and too fast and you will wonder why anyone would bother").

Jamie, a tall skinny Dubliner of 45 with lank pale yellow hair, nicotine-stained fingers and a slightly broken bass-baritone whisper of a voice, had directed two important art-house films about the Dublin working class. He could be caustically funny ("Well, Nica, that would be one of the two worst scenes presented today — had there been another scene presented today"), but always followed any little dig with useful information that improved my work ("You're saying you're very glad to see Judge Brack, but surely you're not. You need to make a list of all the reasons you are not glad, all the problems he presents … and, most important, what you will do to prevent him causing these problems. At the same time, it will be useful to compare ways that the Judge reminds you of your father. These ways are there. You must find them").

Jamie the teacher did this with every student, and things never got really nasty unless someone was lazy. Lazy students usually either left LATF within a season or changed from sluggish wounded martyrs to hard workers.

My professional relationship with Jamie was, apart from childhood osmosis at home, school plays and the Montmartre Cinéma, the bedrock of my training, and supports my work to this day, twenty years later.

Our personal relationship was somewhat harder to navigate, though equally informative — sometimes even equally joyous.

Jamie was a heavy drinker. Which meant that, at some point in his alcohol consumption arc, he would be drunk. He did not drink while teaching (excepting what he called the "Greet the Dawn" shot in the morning), so the best time to sleep with him was before dinner, as *after* dinner would probably be too late and he would be a sodden lump, sound asleep beside me, eau de Jameson's Irish Whiskey coming through the skin of his chest and scenting the room. To maintain school propriety, I always had to leave his rooms before daylight. On Lead Lump Nights, I did this quite early in the evening.

Jamie, long familiar with the problem, would find a way, during play analysis or scene study, to whisper something like "Got something against necrophilia, have ye?" before smiling, squeezing my shoulder, and continuing the general discussion.

When at least semi-sober, he was a wonderful lover, tender, considerate, sensual and capable of being warm, personal and skilled at the same time (as I have learned since, "personal" and "skilled" is a very rare simultaneous combination).

Which brings me to another thing that makes me happy: the glorious, extraordinary, wondrous, magical, complexion-improving, heart-strengthening, disposition-ameliorating and entirely revelatory human female orgasm.

So, long live Jamie Concannon, now dead, who taught me:

1. Scene study.
2. Play and character analysis.
3. Styles of acting.
4. Acting-for-camera, film-shot sizes, and how to shoot out-of-sequence.
5. The relationship of costume to character and how to not wrinkle your costume during long waits in your dressing room.
6. Re-recording your own voice after filming has concluded.
7. Location filming.
8. When to eat when filming. What to eat when filming. When to drink when filming.
9. How to identify crew-members by occupation.
10. With whom you should sleep (if you wish) or not sleep (even if you wish to) during a film shoot.

And

11. Where within yourself you must go in order to come.

Papa, Maman, Jean Marie Carignac, and Mario Zavani (who returned periodically to Maman's life, though far more as a "walker" than an *amour fou*), attended LATF graduation ceremonies. My classmates were pleased to meet them all, and they seemed to enjoy being valued for their actual work, much of which was cited by name — this in a mostly pre-Internet age, when young actors still knew films and plays because they'd actually *seen* them.

My classmates were clearly happiest to meet Carignac, whose Cinémathèque had been praised and discussed in class. Carignac, looking up at their eager faces and turning slowly, in the fashion of a hand-held camera shot, in order to address each one personally, said, in English, that he would like very much for them to apply to the Cinémathèque, but that all of those who attend "must have the French."

At our dinner, at a quietly elegant Lebanese restaurant in Bayswater, I wrapped myself in the warmth of my parents' pride and had my first "equals" conversation with Jean Marie Carignac. We discussed the differences between black-and-white and colour film. Papa, whose business was light and shadow, joined this discussion. Maman, a bit bored by this discourse and seeing no one to whom she could table-hop (always possible in Paris), murmured with Mario, pretending to be still interested in him.

I had invited Jamie Concannon to join us after the ceremonies. He replied that he could not, "on this special night, publicly favour one student over the rest of the class. I need to go out with the largest pack of 'em. But I would love to stop and raise a glass with you all. Tell me where you're going and I'll stop by later."

While we were having after-dinner coffee and brandy, Jamie arrived, wearing his battered cigarette-wounded tweed jacket, faded jeans and long, wound-round-and-round beige hand-knitted scarf — looking, as ever, like a glamorous scarecrow. He shook hands with Maman, Papa, Mario and (most reverentially) with Carignac, each handshake involving holding one of their hands in two of his. He congratulated my parents on their work, proclaiming himself a long-time admirer. He praised Mario's most recent film, which he'd seen "just a week ago, in Chelsea."

I knew this was true. We'd seen the film together. He hadn't liked Mario in it. "Too much self-love," he'd said.

With Carignac, I got to see Jamie being an acolyte, something I was fairly certain rarely happened. Jamie scrunched into himself to be as small as possible and spoke even more whisper-softly than usual, in French, using the word "Maître." The clear admiration of a serious and respected "Maître Anglais" illuminated Carignac from within. Years fell away as he animatedly held forth on matters cinematic. We all listened. Maman and I shared a small smile of remembrance and she mouthed the words *Le Cochon qui Danse.*

We finished our drinks, Jamie having two tumblers of Jameson's while the rest of us sipped our brandy. Even my father, who had the Swedish gift for drinking buckets without appearing drunk, was quite content to consume two glasses of red wine and one Rémy Martin cognac.

When we'd paid our bill and stood to go, Jamie said again, straightforwardly without fawning, that he was honoured to meet everyone. He congratulated my parents on "a splendid genetic success in Nica," kissed me on the cheek, whispered that he'd see me later at his rooms, and took off, turning once, at the door of the restaurant, to wave and smile.

I was walking my guests to their nearby hotel when Maman lightly tugged me to walk alongside her, behind the men.

"How old is he, Dominique?"

"How old is who, Maman?"

She tilted her head and raised an eyebrow, as I knew she would.

"You know who."

"About forty-five. I've never asked."

"He is at *least* forty-five. And an alcoholic. He is charming, and clearly very fine in his work, and in what he has given to you as an artist. But, as a man, he is wrong for you. You are young. You are about to embark on a wonderful career, I believe. Please do not waste yourself on … unlikely people."

I looked at Carignac and Mario Zavani walking in front of us. Two of my mother's many Beloved Unlikelies. Maman followed my gaze as I noted that "We go where we go, Maman, and it is wonderful ... until it isn't. Please don't worry. Like you, I want to do my work and ... will not stay in a bad place. Even if I accidentally stumble into a bad place."

"I see. Good. Fine."

When I got to Jamie's rooms he was in deep sleep, a glass and an almost empty bottle of Jameson's on his bed-table. I gathered together the few belongings I kept there and wrote him a note expressing love and thanks, along with my parents' Paris and Stockholm addresses. I sat on the edge of his bed, realising I knew almost nothing about Jamie Concannon that wasn't related to our shared work or transitory moments of pleasure. I knew we were done and already missed him, even though I'd believed for months that this would be the night we were done. And that it would probably be less than a week before my replacement was in his bed. I was even fairly certain who that replacement would be: Shelina Patel.

I had seen her choose him at the welcoming session for new students. As I had done a year earlier. It had taken me almost five months to actualise my choice; Shelina was surer, bolder, and not the daughter of a woman who was girlishly thunderstruck by a Grand Amour at least once a year. I wanted to open a door, but not a constantly *revolving* door.

Luck and some primal instinct had allowed me to have my sexual debut with what the clinical types called a "serial monogamist." And now, as with serial films, I could see the word "fin" on our shared screen. As in the cinéma, it was always expected. Ours was neither a happy nor a sad ending. It was the only possible ending.

Jamie's battered but fine-boned face looked, in sleep, like the almost albino version of an El Greco saint. His mouth was slightly opened and pale fine baby hair fell across his eyes. I brushed back the hair, kissed him lightly on the forehead, placed his key on the bed-table, and tiptoed out the door and into streetlight-sparkly London summer rain.

As a graduation present, Maman had brought me a contract for a French film in which we would play together. The director, Charles Aubin, had known me since I was born. Maman showed him the audition-reel that all LATF students had to make, and, said Maman, "Charles accepted you almost at once, Dominique, with great pleasure. He liked very much your screen presence and your acting, but what decided him was your superb rendition, in English, of 'Falling in Love Again'. He wants you to sing it in the film."

The film, *Les Deux Médecins Roberge,* was a popular success in France, garnering César film awards for both Maman and me. We had portrayed mother and daughter doctors, the younger of whom was terminally ill ("It is superb to die in film, Dominique; it makes you very sympatique and everyone knows you are a serious artist because you are willing to look terrible and also die").

The success of *Les Deux Médecins Roberge* and the twin César awards led to a spate of other French films, for both Maman and me, including a second duo film with Charles Aubin (which did acceptably but nowhere nearly as well as *Les Deux Médecins*). I also made films, in solid roles, two of them leads, in Italy and in what used to be the Soviet Union.

While in the USSR, I attended an homage to the films of Sergei Eisenstein, and was once again in a dark room with my first love, Nikolai Tcherkhassov. In my speech honouring Eisenstein I told the Moscow audience, with the aid of a translator, about my great childhood fantasy affair: Maman, Papa, The Cinéma, Clothilde Lussier, Marlene Dietrich et al. The story received wonderful applause, as well as sympathetic laughter.

Carignac was also there. Over eighty years old, he taught less frequently at the Cinémathèque but was often asked to attend homages given by film centres and festivals throughout the world, and was himself often the honouree. On these occasions, there would be a screening of *Le Boulot de Ma Mère.* Sometimes Maman and I were also in attendance, and I would see the face of my mother when she was 19. It was startling how much like her I'd come to look. I even had some of Maman's reflexive mannerisms, particularly pursing my lips and holding my chin between thumb and index finger and raising then lowering my eyes (my father's blue eyes) before telling another character that I did not want to do something.

My twenties were a good period for me, and for my parents. We were all working, and most of our projects turned out well. I was becoming a popular European film actress, filming constantly, receiving good reviews.

Sexually, I fell into film actor's habits: becoming involved with someone connected with whatever project I was doing. And, usually, becoming uninvolved when the project ended. There were exceptions to this pattern: a few two-nighters (*one*-nighters being, somehow, insulting — sleep with me twice and you can go if you wish. Once, only once, made me feel undesirable. This quirk made me laugh but also concerned me. Desirability was so important to Maman. I had not wanted it to matter to me. But it did).

One relationship lasted longer than the length of a film-shoot: Eddie Avakian was sound director for a number of my films. From the start we were good together, sharing tastes in music, food, sex and humour. His gymnastic background, thick straight black hair and strong-featured big face made him look like a highly evolved comic-book jungle hero. His French-Armenian family liked me and I liked them. We lived together on the *Marie-Claudette,* his damp but wonderful barge on the Seine. After three years, and some film-driven separations, Eddie asked me to marry him. I could've married Eddie. Perhaps I should've married Eddie. But almost no one I knew had "a marriage;" they had "a first marriage," "a second marriage," etc. I saw no point in it — all that paperwork and negotiation, only to do what you would do without all that paperwork and negotiation.

Eddie was angry that I declined to marry him. I said I didn't blame him for being angry. This made him even angrier. He stopped speaking to me. I accepted a badly-written but long-scheduled film in Russia, dreading bad food, pink water, corseted heavy costumes, scalp-sweating wigs, and people constantly practising being entrepreneurial through a black market habit filter.

I did revel in the vodka-generated open-armed full-throated singing that happened in the bar in Pushkin Square after every shooting day.

The crew, delighted by my interest, taught me Romany and Vladimir Visotsky songs. I sang well in Russian and sometimes did Vodka-fuelled dances with Dima, the Russian sound director, with whom I also sometimes went home. I missed Eddie. In fact, I probably only slept with Dima because he was an attractive man who did the same work as Eddie. And I'd slept with Eddie, the first time, because of Room Tone.

3 Room Tone

As deeply as I love doing the work of film acting, my favourite moment on any set, from my first job to the present, is Room Tone. At that moment, on the last day of filming, the sound director shouts, "Quiet, everyone. Quiet on the set. Complete silence please. Room Tone!"

Upon hearing this cry, every human on the set becomes completely still, save for breathing. The sound of the room, the room's tone, is then recorded.

Technically, this is done so that if, after filming has concluded, you have to re-record lines of dialogue, the sometimes almost imperceptible but, in fact, completely individuated sound of the room will remain the same throughout the filmed scene.

That's the technical reason, but for me Room Tone has always been the closest that film people, as an interwoven collective of individuals, will come to shared meditation. Together and silent, all our quotidian fears, anxieties, and petty grievances are stilled, lest they somehow jostle the focused harmony of the Room Tone.

Life is filled with adventure, sensation, acquired knowledge, wonder, magic, beauty, laughter, and joy. It is also filled with noise, pushing, shoving, betrayal, suspicion, disappointment, horror, weeping, stupidity, violence, jealousy, and petty cruelty.

Except for the time of Room Tone. Room Tone is, for a moment or two, humans at our best. Quiet. Listening together to the sound of the room — a sound of which each of us is a breathing part. Room Tone is perfect.

4 Big Face, Small Voice

PRIMARILY A CINEMA CREATURE, I made my professional theatre debut, at 28, in a Paris production of Strindberg's *Miss Julie*, which received mixed reviews. It was a large theatre. My voice, praised in film for being "throaty and sexy" (as Papa had predicted it would one day be), was too small to carry properly in the cavernous space. The theatre work I'd done at LATF, in a far smaller theatre, had gone well. That success, plus the arrogance of youth, had led me to believe that if I worked hard, fully played my character, and moved well in the right costumes, all would be perfect.

In order to see "a normal performance, when all the fuss of first night nonsense has settled down," Papa flew in from Stockholm a week into the run. We sat backstage after the show, sharing the Christmas aquavit he'd brought. He confirmed what I had begun to learn — the critics were correct; if I wanted to do theatre I needed to either strengthen my voice or play only in small theatres. He also said Maman, years earlier, had the same problem and, not liking negative reviews, never did another play. I laughed.

"Well, Papa, I don't like bad critiques either — *quelle surprise!* — but I would like to do plays from time to time. I will build my voice … at some point. When the film schedule permits."

5 Nica Goes to Hollywood

WHEN THE CALL CAME FROM HOLLYWOOD, Papa was cautious, Maman was thrilled, and I was terrified. The call wasn't from a film-maker, but from an agent, Philip Rosenthal, who was "captivated" by my film work and wondered if I had "American representation." If I did not have this representation, he went on to write, "PRA, a well-respected international agency (see enclosed clients' list), would be most interested in meeting with you at the earliest mutual convenience. If you are unable to come to Los Angeles at this time, I would be happy to come to Paris (as anyone in his or her right mind is always happy to come to Paris)."

The family gathered at the Montparnasse apartment to discuss this over a quiet dinner of *coq au vin* and good wine.

I did not have *any* "representation." Neither did most actors in most non-anglophone European capitals. We were a community of colleagues and usually negotiated for ourselves. Maman said our system, while "warmer and more honest," was "impossible if one wishes to have a larger career, a career in English." She'd always regretted "not properly expanding my opportunity base when I was young enough to do so. This is your opportune moment, Dominique. You must take it!"

Papa said I should explore this new possibility, but that, if I wished to meet with M. Rosenthal, I must go to Los Angeles. "I know Los Angeles, Nica. It is … very different to any place you have been. You need to see the place, meet the people, see how they work. If your Mister Rosenthal comes here and is charming, if you like him, you will sign a contract in Paris and then find yourself in … an Oz of many wizards, with no clickable red shoes to return you home."

"Oh, Bo!" Maman exclaimed, "you are always so pessimist. Dominique would only be agreeing to have representation. She does not have to accept work she does not wish to do. PRA is a very powerful agency. Their roster includes many international stars, including (she studied the list, counting names with her shiny copper-coloured fingernail) one-two-three-four-five French artists and one-two-three Swedes."

"Åsa Hansen is Danish. And they've made her change her name to 'Osa'."

"For God's sake, Bo. There is no 'Å' in the English alphabet. This does not make the Americans evil people."

"Of course they are not 'evil people'. I never said they are evil people. They are people that do not like to learn how to pronounce anything. And sometimes, after the entire fanfare, absolutely nothing happens. Mylene DuMaurier went there. They changed her name to Mimi, gave her all sorts of publicity, took lots of pictures. She said they all praised her acting, her ass and her Gallic insouciance but, in three years, she did two dreadful films and a handful of boring television shows, and then came home without any money and had to do a stupid Italian Téléroman to get out of debt."

I sipped my wine, knowing from years of experience that it was best to let these debates settle a bit before entering them — even, perhaps *especially*, if you are the actual subject of the debate.

That more settled time arrived during coffee and cognac. I agreed with both my parents: they would pay my way to Los Angeles. I would see the Hollywoodians in their natural habitat and, if I thought I could work there, would sign with PRA and give it a go.

Philip Rosenthal was not called Philip. Everyone who spoke of him in Hollywood (and most everyone in Hollywood spoke of him) called him Cuffs. Cuffs Rosenthal. He was, I was told, called "Cuffs" because he had a habit, in conversation, of shooting his fisted hands out in front of him, exposing the white cuffs and gold cufflinks of his expensive shirts.

Toni Helfman, his personal secretary, explained this to me when I first visited the PRA offices, whispering confidentially that "He does not call himself 'Cuffs'. He calls himself 'Philip' and expects you to address him as Philip. He hates the name Cuffs. It's a bit like Bugsy Siegel."

"Bugsy? Seagull?"

"Yeah. Famous American gangster. Philip isn't any sort of gangster or anything. Bugsy shot people who called him Bugsy. Philip has, to my knowledge, never shot anybody for calling him Cuffs. But he does hate it."

"Oh. Certainly. I will never call Monsieur Rosenthal … that other word. And (I laughed lightly, with what I hoped was Gallic insouciance) *you* should be careful not to say 'Bugsy', yes?"

"No. Bugsy's dead. Somebody shot him."

Toni buzzed M. Rosenthal. A slightly high-pitched male voice responded.

"Yeah, Toni."

"Miss Lind is here for you, Mister Rosenthal."

"Great! Please send her in."

Philip Rosenthal's office was the size of a luxury hotel room (I would later refer to it as Le Grand Hotel Rosenthal). Its floor-to-ceiling windows revealed automobile traffic weaving in all directions on a complex snake-cluster of roads; hills, sky and blinding white sunlight, with a smattering of black or terra cotta coloured towers pushing up here and there.

Directly in front of the central window was a high, square dark wood pedestal ascended or descended via three wraparound steps of the same wood. Atop the pedestal sat a large oak desk, tastefully cluttered with small photos in silver, gold or crystal frames, plus pencils and pens in a red and black leather cylinder. Behind this desk sat Philip Rosenthal, sunlight glinting off his tanned and shaved head.

"Hello, Miss Lind! Welcome to Los Angeles!"

He stood. I noted that he favoured the black and grey pinstripe suits and dark red silk ties I'd already seen in my two days among what my host, William McLean, a director who'd worked with my father, called "the power-lunchers."

Philip/Cuffs walked very quickly around his desk and, in black leather running shoes, descended the three steps at a lightning pace, holding his right hand out stiffly in welcome, smiling a sunny close-lipped smile. He did not offer his hand to be shaken in the usual American fashion, but scooted into a handsome black leather chair with a very fat pillow, simultaneously gesturing to a matching chair, with a far thinner cushion, in which I understood immediately that I was to sit. I sat.

All of this took about thirty seconds. In this brief moment of motion there was only a flash of the reason for the pedestal, the high desk and the fast-forward manoeuvre: Philip Cuffs Rosenthal was about the same size as Jean Marie Carignac.

Unlike Carignac, who was completely at home within his skin and his size, M. Rosenthal was trying, I thought, completely fascinated, to move so quickly that I would not find out he was short. Or, at the least, I would witness his shortness as briefly as possible. I remembered what my father had said. Hollywood is an Oz of many wizards. I was meeting my first Hollywood Oz wizard.

Still smiling, gradually revealing perfectly crafted very white teeth, he looked at me with small bright brown-button eyes and said, "So glad you could come, Nica. How was your flight?"

I returned his smile, trying not to look as startled as I was by the sprint, saying, "Merci, Monsieur Rosenthal (Maman had said 'a smattering of French words excites Americans. They think it's sexy'). My flight was … uneventful. The best sort, I think."

"Yeah, me too. You a nervous flyer?"

"Yes, I was this time. It was my first very long flight. In Europe, all the flights are (Oh God, I thought, I should not say the word 'short') … brief. Everywhere is so near to everywhere else."

He laughed, a mirthless ha-ha-ha.

"Yeah. That's one of the great things about Europe, Nica. One of many great things. The only reason I live here is because this is where all the action is."

6 All the Action

1. My first L.A. job was in the "leading role" of "Fifi La Foxe" in *Critters in Space,* a ToonLand feature film. Fifi was an extraterrestrial fox with a curvaceous figure. *Critters* starred Billy Dallas as "Wolfie," the wolf who loved me.

2. Billy introduced me to cocaine but it made me sneeze lot and caused my nose to leak constantly, so I gave it up before it got to the "You tell those limpdick bastards they better not fuck with me or I'll have 'em whacked out!" stage. Billy Dallas had been at that stage for some years, as had a number of ladies and gentlemen in Hollywood.

3. *Critters* was nominated for a Best Animated Feature Award. Billy and I were also nominated, as was Al Feldner, for writing and singing the theme song, "If You'll Be Good to Me, I'll Be Good to You," which featured a vicious lyric and an exquisite melody that would make you cry if you didn't speak English.

4. I did a film with Shawn Flannery, the great Anglo-Irish character actor, who'd been in film since the silent era. He and his wife Mary became friends to me. I told them I'd seen Shawn's early films at the Cinémathèque in Paris. The Flannerys had a small and lovely beach house in Santa Monica "near where Marion Davies used to live. Used to see Hearst and Chaplin and all of 'em comin' an' goin' all the time. Was invited a few times as well, weren't we, Mary mine?"

The Flannerys were like an oasis for me. It was wonderful to slap up a meal at their place, watch the amazing Pacific sunset, and then see videos of Shawn's films as he progressed from leading man to character actor.

Our film, *Boots,* was really about a ten-year-old boy and his blind cat.

Shawn died in his sleep three days after we finished filming. The Flannerys had three dogs and no children. I took Mary to the funeral at Forest Lawn, where we held each other up and, without noise (I'd been trained; Mary was a quiet woman) wept. The dogs, all sweet mongrels, held on leads by Asuncion, the Flannery's housekeeper, being neither quiet nor particularly trained, howled.

Shawn, who'd played the leading boy's Irish grandfather, was nominated, posthumously, for a Best Supporting Actor Award. I'd played Shawn's son's second wife, a German gold-digger. I was not nominated. Nor should I have been. I never really inhabited the role and my German accent was too French.

Mary Flannery asked me to accompany her to the ceremony and, if "Shaneen" won anything, to please accept on his behalf.

Shawn, the sentimental favourite, did win. I stood on a round platform, wearing a shimmering gold sequined floor-length sheath that had belonged to my mother, having climbed five banisterless stairs in what were still called, in Hollywoodian self-reference, "Joan Crawford Fuck-Me Pumps."

I told about how Shawn had to change the spelling of his name when he came to Hollywood, because Famous Players said everyone would call him "Seen." I told how the Flannerys were one of, perhaps, four couples I'd ever seen who truly loved each other. To keep Mary from weeping, I ended with how "Shawn Flannery always said the most important part of a woman's body is the legs, because that's what you need to run away from all the creepy guys out here." I took off my alpine strappy-sandal heels and said, "Slainte, my dear Shaneen. I'm gonna run away now, to run back to your beloved Mary and give her your prize, because it's a grand t'ing, innit?" I held up the award, shouted, as Shawn always did, in the Stage Irish he said they loved in Hollywood, "Bless ye, me darlin', for the angel that y'are!" In stockinged feet, sandals hooked over my index finger, I then ran back to Mary and gave her the award as cameras whirred and popped.

7 My Rack

A WEEK AFTER THE AWARDS, Augie Particelli, Cuffs Rosenthal's Associate Agent, telephoned and asked me to meet him at The Burgerie, a trendy lunch hangout in Beverley Hills. "Philip wants to share some thoughts with you. Unfortunately, he is in Florida, so he has asked me to bring these thoughts to you, at a mutually convenient time, of course. By the way, Philip thought you looked absolutely beautiful and that your speech at the Awards was totally delightful."

Absolutely beautiful, totally delightful, and in sensible running shoes, expensively faded jeans and a skin-tight teeshirt over my small breasts and large nipples, I met Augie at the Burgerie later that same day.

He was feeding his already St. Nicholas-like belly with an enormous sandwich (even by American standards) called the HumungoBurger with Everything. The wide smile inside his moon-face showed the same hyperwhite perfect teeth as those of his boss, and of most everyone in Hollywood — with the possible exception of the homeless people (some of whom did have lovely teeth from before they were homeless).

I ordered a tomato and mushroom salad and a Perrier, after assuring the always diffident Augie that I really, honestly, yes I was sure, did not want a beer or a glass of wine or even a cocktail.

Within five minutes I learned that the tight teeshirt was probably a mistake.

"Listen kid," he began, "Philip thinks you're just great! Terrific. That's why he asked you to come in from Paris. That's why he signed you. As you know, as *everybody* knows, PRA has a very exclusive list. And we are very proud to have you on that list. Very proud. And Philip is talking you up everywhere. We all are. We know you have a fine career in Europe and we believe you can be even bigger here ... but we're having a problem. Not a *huge* problem, kid. You're working, particularly with animated and commercials and some television. But only one feature. Philip thinks ... well, he thinks it's a rack problem."

"A rack problem?"

Augie fingered the gold cross around his neck. He looked embarrassed for a moment and then recovered. His face looked like the faces of doctors in films, doctors speaking to terminal patients. He nodded three times.

"Look kid, this is awkward. I'm old enough to be your father. And Philip is old enough to be mine. Philip wants you to have a rack job. Have your breasts made bigger. He says he can't sell a French girl with a small rack, with small breasts. Not in a town where all the good-looking young girls, girls who look like you, have ..."

I got up and walked out of the Burgerie, moving almost as fast as Cuffs Rosenthal did when hiding his height. There was a ticket, as there was most every day, on my rented red Toyota. I yanked the ticket from under the windscreen wiper, tore it into many pieces and threw the pieces into the air, shouting *"EncuLAY, ollywooood!"* I then got into the car and headed to Malibu.

I drove out Sunset Boulevard to the Pacific Coast Highway. At the "T" where Sunset ends and the Highway begins, I looked to my left at the hanging gardens of the Self-Realisation Fellowship. Self-Realisation. Myself had just been asked to realise that I, she, my self, had tits too tiny for a big-screen career in California. I turned right, self-realising every swear word I knew in French, Swedish, Italian and English, plus a few in Russian. I rolled down the window of the Toyota and shouted into the blue sea and up at the blue sky.

"Balloongas! Big balloongas! I've seen those balloongas my Oz wizard wants me to have. You lie down, they don't. The solution moves. They have to be redone. I hate them! I hate this entire damn thing! Except for the sea, the sky, Mexican food, and enormous fruit. Enormous fruit? Oh God, the fruit has probably all had a fruit job!" And then, being just another crazed Californian, fearless in her car, I shouted, "Cuffs!

They call you 'Cuffs', you Academy Award sized Boob-freak! Cuffs! Cuffs! Cuffs! There! I said it! Cuffs! Your name is Cuffs! Now have me killed, you little fucker!"

It was good to scream, good that I was alone, and good that there were no witnesses.

I parked the car and went for a walk on the beach. Between two large rocks, I took off my teeshirt and looked at my small rocks. I thought they were lovely. I cupped them in my hands.

"I love you, mes petits jolie tétons. We're in this together! All for two and two for all! No one will take the inflaters' knife to you! Not ever!"

Then I looked around, laughing.

"Oh God, I'm topless in Malibu talking to my tits. Shawn Flannery was right — if you're not careful, Hollywood will start seeming like real life, and that can make a body crazy. Go home, Nica Lind. Go home, Dominique Lindskog."

By the time I'd driven back to my little guesthouse on Sunset Plaza drive, I had decided. A firm decision. I would return, as immediately as possible, to Europe, where I had a career, a family, a life. And two perfect breasts.

I parked the car in its assigned space alongside the large Georgian-style mansion that belonged to my landlord, Karl Freund, an old gentleman who composed film scores.

Mister Freund ("Please. Call me Karl. 'Mister Freund' makes me feel so old") was eighty-five and had been a boyfriend of Tilly Duber's in pre-Hitler Weimar Germany. Like Freddy Hirsch, Karl had fled the Nazis by coming to Hollywood. Film scores and popular songs in the 1930s through the 1940s made him rich and he invested in cheap land. The cheap land became expensive real estate and Karl became richer still.

He'd never married, liked dating "pretty little chickadees" and "taking junkets" to Las Vegas. Mrs. Fleck, his live-in nurse, was a sweet middle-aged woman who would accompany him to Vegas, where she would stay close by, playing slot machines or seeing shows, while pretending not to know him unless he became dizzy or short of breath.

On the two occasions where this happened (one dizziness, one s.o.b.), the Pretty Little Chickadees were a bit startled, though probably also relieved when a large woman shooed them away and ministered to the nice old man who had been buying them things.

When Maman told the Carignac Gang I was going to L.A. Tilly suggested that her old friend Freund had a guesthouse. The two-storey poolhouse was perfect for me.

Karl's eyes tended to light up with thoughts of my potential Little Chickadee-ness, so I insisted on paying rent and, if I were alone, would wave quickly, smile broadly, and run like hell when I passed his window. He would tap on the window with his cane and beckon me in. I would make inane "got to run" gestures and mouthings, and then mime a telephone and point to him. Fortunately, there was a small armada of Chickadees wriggling about in the house most of the time, as well as Mrs. Fleck, so I did not feel guilty about my solo-visit-avoidance.

Scooting past the mansion and pool, I heard my phone ringing. I opened the sliding glass doors and picked up the receiver of the slippery white telephone (It was called a Princess. The Americans have a complex relationship to royalty).

"Hello. Nica Lind here."

It was Augie Particelli. He was so sorry. He hadn't wanted to discuss my rack. He, Augie, had two daughters and wouldn't want some guy discussing their racks. Mister Rosenthal had insisted that he, Augie, discuss my rack because he, Mister Rosenthal, didn't want to discuss my rack, or anybody's rack, but thought I was going to need a bigger rack but now I didn't need a big rack because "you got *Cimarron,* kiddo, and the money is *great!* Fifty thousand per episode for thirteen and then we renegotiate. They really want you. You're the only one they want. They'll look again if you can't do it but it's you they want. Your own trailer. Car and driver. The whole nine. Philip said you wanted to go back to Paris and they doubled everything to keep you here and …"

"Augie?"

"Yeah, kid."

"I *do* want to go back to Paris. Me and my little rack."

"Forget about your rack, kid. *You* got *Cimarron!*"

8 Cimarron

PEOPLE FROM OTHER PLACES spend years in Hollywood. Many stay because each time they are definitely leaving, someone who is supposed to know such things says that something amazing, brilliant and career-transforming is about to happen in the days, weeks or, maximum, months to follow.

The most important thing to know if you are going to Hollywood as an actor is this: if you've had any credible success (and sometimes even if you've none) people will say Yes to you. All the time. About anything you want to do. Everyone may not say yes every time, but someone will say yes to anything you ask about. Each request gets at least one yes, and some things get enough yesses to yes the universe until the end of time. Or so it will seem to the hopeful hapless yessee.

99% of the yesses are just Hollywoodspeak for no. 1% are actual yesses.

And yes, I was being offered an enormous amount of money and extras to play the female lead, every week, in *Cimarron*.

I rang off with Augie and telephoned my father in Stockholm. I told him everything that had happened, up to "and I've been offered the female lead on an important television series here." He listened quietly, murmuring an occasional "mm" except when I told him about the request for an augmented rack. He then, atypically, shouted, "Bloody savage bastards! If they come anywhere near my daughter with a knife I will personally …"

"Papa, Papa. It's all right. I will never do this. I was going to come home immediately because they'd even suggested it."

"Good. As you should do. Please come home. You are loved here, as you are."

"I know, Papa ... but they've offered me *Cimarron.*"

"I don't care if they've offered you Monaco. Please come home, Nica. You don't belong there."

I then told him about the money and perks being proposed, and that it was only for thirteen weeks' work.

There was silence. Then he asked if I were sure about the thirteen weeks. I told him I would see the contract the following day and would only sign for thirteen weeks.

Another silence. Then, "All right, Nica. Thirteen weeks. Then you take your enormous pile of American dollars and come home, yes?"

"Yes."

"Good. ... Nica?"

"Yes, Papa?"

"You have ... a lovely chest. The same chest as your mother. I love you."

"*Cimarron*" was actually called *You Mean This **Isn't** Cimarron?!* It took place in Vaca Grande (Big Cow), a small wild-west town, two blocks long, next to the larger wild-west town of Cimarron. The show, set in the 1890s, was a parody of old American frontier westerns, with serious contemporary themes interwoven in the sometimes dark, sometimes surreal comedy. The writers were a Scottish couple, Mari and Iain Mac Innes, and the director was Danny Wechsler. They'd all won numerous awards for eccentrically funny and politically risky comedy-dramas (the Californians, bless them, had invented a word for this: *Cimarron* would be, as the L.A. theatrical establishment described the trio's entire body of work, a Dramady).

I "took a meeting" the following day at PRA. Philip Rosenthal sat in his chair, behind his desk, atop his pedestal. The two producers and the director sat on a fat-pillow black leather sofa, one level down from the pedestal. I sat on a fat-cushioned black leather chair. Augie Particelli filled a thin-pillow black leather chair. Toni Helfman sat behind the non-pedestal group, at a little desk, recording the proceedings and making notes. The bar in the right wall was open in case anyone wanted coffee, liquor or mineral water.

It was agreed that I would portray Lili Dangereuse, singer and femme fatale at The Paranoid Coyote, a saloon owned by Hacking Koffman, Viennese barkeep and Freudian Psychiatrist of Vaca Grande.

For my portrayal — someone similar to Madeleine Kahn in *Blazing Saddles* playing Marlene Dietrich in *Destry Rides Again* — I would receive more money in one week than I'd ever made in a year. And, after thirteen weeks, if the show was a success, they would have to renegotiate my contract. I said nothing of it to Philip Rosenthal and the others, but I would not renegotiate. Not at any price. After thirteen weeks I would get the hell out of Hollywood and go back to doing serious work in Europe.

*You Mean This **Isn't** Cimarron?* was an enormous success. An enormous American success. It was number one in the television ratings for three years, and never dropped below number four. We all won awards. I recorded albums: *Lili Dangereuse Sings Marlene Dietrich* (very successful) and *Nica Lind — Songs of Paris* (not so successful. The record executives said it was because I used my own name instead of "Lili Dangereuse"). We had little action dolls that represented our characters. We were photographed from every angle, in various states of undress and stability, at every possible location. We were interviewed, quoted, misquoted, lied to, lied for, and lied about.

My thirteen weeks lasted eight years, destroying the possibility of my portraying anyone in America other than Lili Dangereuse. We all kept signing new contracts, for insane amounts of money. People bitched about whatever actors bitch about, but nobody left except Chang Wu, who played Wing Ding, the ancient Chinese cook at the Paranoid Coyote. Chang only left because he had a heart attack at eighty-four and died. The year before he died, he starred in a wonderful *Cimarron* episode where he told the story of his parents, who opened up the Rocky Mountains by having dynamite strapped to their bodies by their white bosses. "They did not know," Chang said softly (as Wing Ding), "that they would become part of the mountain."

Chang had also been a celebrated singer of Chinese Opera, so the team wrote an episode where Wing Ding tries to introduce that musical form to the Paranoid Coyote Saloon. The Sheriff of Vaca Grande, Deadeye Derek Dunavan (who lives in a room above the saloon), protests, insisting that the classic form sounds like "two cats mating in an alley." My character, Lili, loves the sound. "She is so free, zis sound, so abandonée!" The sequence ends with Lili and Wing Ding howling together while everyone flees except Socks the Saloon cat (called "Sucks" by the misanthropic Deadeye), who sings along. Comet, the saloon dog, who is 17 years old, sleeps through it, as she does through everything.

We frequently felt as if we were caged with crazy people. In fact, the only crazy person with whom we were caged was Gareth Willett, but though he was only one man, Gareth, who starred as Deadeye Derek Dunavan, had enough crazy happening to more than replicate the craziness quota of any small madhouse. And an equal amount of talent. On our first day of shooting, I watched him transform, as needed, three or four times, and nicknamed him "Loup Garou." He accepted the name at once, though only from me (as Danny Wechsler found out, in front of cast and crew, when he tried to use it), never asking what it meant.

9 Gareth Willett ~ Any Small Madhouse

GARETH'S CORE PROBLEM WAS NOT MADNESS. It was drink —
or, more accurately, the things that caused him to drink.

He'd been some sort of star, initially in the UK, since he was 15. And
as beautiful as Michelangelo's David. And from a working class
Liverpool family that still called him "Our Kid." Their kid had believed,
since he was a kid, that real men were prizefighters, betting-shop book-
makers, factory workers, and footballers. Actors, who wore makeup
and costumes and pretended to be other people, were girls. Not effem-
inate men — male girls. When his alcohol content was somewhere
between Fully Pissed and Fall Down, he would expound on his male
girlness, declaring that "gay men are far less fucked up than ol' Gareth
here. They've got it clear. They're men who like men. Me, I'm a girl who
likes girls and can't even be a proper dyke. Not without cutting off
my dick. Soooo, here I be, as you see me — a big pretty failed dyke with
a big ugly dick."

As the *Cimarron* gang had learned, no sane person could argue with
Gareth about this. Arguing with Gareth was never a sanity-enhancing
option on any subject. In GarethLand, male actors were girls. Chicks
with Dicks. Pretty Little Stars. Before every shot, every shot, he would
mutter, his face twisted into a grimace of disgust, "Pretty Little Star is
ready to twinkle now."

And then he would do that: he would twinkle, laugh, cry, shout,
wink or whisper. Whatever was required. And he would do it all wonderfully. Gareth Willett, the most entirely fucked-up human being I'd
ever seen (in a profession with no dearth of such creatures), was a great
actor. To be inside a scene with him was to be fully doing the work

that is called acting. If you engaged with his passion, bravery, imagination and mad eyeballs you could do nothing less. Actors, whether they'd done it for years or had never done it before (and probably never would again, even if they became stars), were at the top of their game when they acted with Gareth Willett.

When the scene was over and the crew was setting up the next shot, Gareth, already half-drunk, would turn to Danny Wechsler, our director, and say, "Little Girl was brilliant! Wasn't she, Mister Man?" before pushing past us to wait in his dressing room trailer until he was called for the next shot.

Gareth's drink trajectory meant that we could only shoot his scenes until three in the afternoon, maximum, though we could prop his inert body in a chair for a shot taken over his shoulder. It was strange to play a scene talking to his closed eyes and slack drooling lips. Strange but not impossible. Having started my sexual life with a drinking man, I knew how to talk to the inert, so I did most of those scenes. It was also true that when the familiar voice awakened Gareth for a moment, he would see that it was me, feel safe, and sink into drunken sleep again, smiling his version of the same smile Jamie Concannon would offer before passing out. The "I love you, I'm sorry, I'm gone" smile.

Watching the dailies, Gareth saw me seeing him. Danny Wechsler was concerned about Gareth's possible response to, essentially, being used as a prop. He needn't have worried. Gareth, who'd always been sweet with me, became devoted.

And further engaged with me as an actor. He asked Danny if we could do an episode about Deadeye's drinking. Mari and Iain wrote the episode.

The episode was only Deadeye and Lili.

The saloon is closed. Deadeye is clearing the bar counter, drinking all the dregs as he does so. Lili comes down the stairs, on her way around to behind the saloon building to her room upstairs and at the back. She tells Deadeye that mixing drinks will make holes in his guts.

"Like bullet holes," Deadeye says, "except, with bullet holes, blood pours out and men, vicious fearless men, look so surprised. They all do that. They're drawing a loaded gun. I'm drawing a loaded gun. And yet when they're shot, they look surprised. Well, Miss Lili, one day every kind of booze is gonna start pouring out of my gut-holes and, if you're near to see it, will you tell me if I look surprised?"

Deadeye gets drunker and drunker as he tells the story of his England-to-Vaca Grande life. All the hopes. All the plans. His "wonderful mum, who's carried three generations of drunks upstairs to bed, singin' 'God Save the King'."

Finally Deadeye passes out and Lili carries him upstairs to his room, singing *"La Marseillaise."*

That episode also won big annual television awards. Gareth never went to award shows (in fact, was contractually obligated not to), but taped a charming acceptance speech "should we be fortunate in finding favour with you all").

He said Mari, Iain and Danny were brilliant, "almost as brilliant as our crew," and that "the support and love and talent beamed at me at all times by the extraordinary Nica Lind as Lili Dangereuse inspired this performance and the idea for it."

Gareth using the word "love" in his acceptance speech caused massive tabloid speculation about our being "a new two." We'd both ended friendly dalliances with others (his with Miss Somewhere, mine with a Dutch actor doing a series on the same lot as *Cimarron*), so were, in the eyes of those who'd never met either of us, "a sure bet."

After a night shoot in manufactured rain, Gareth walked me to my black Jaguar. He leaned against the car, smiling shyly.

"So, we're a couple, are we?"

"Apparently."

He rested his hand lightly alongside my face.

"Listen, my girl, I will never touch you. I will never touch you … because I love you. Anything I could give ye naked is so much less than I give ye now … and that ain't much."

"It's a lot, Gareth."

"No it's not. But it's all I've got."

"That's why it's a lot."

He took my keys, opened the car door, handed back the keys.

"You're a great lady, Frenchy."

"Nica. I'm Nica. 'Frenchy' is Lili Dangereuse."

"Nica. Nica is a great lady. Nica created Frenchy."

"Exactement. That is exactly right. Nica created Lili Dangereuse."

"I know, my darling. I know how this acting thing works. I work it."

I returned his face touch and then got in the car.

"Do you need a ride, Loup Garou?"

"No, Roly's here. He's like a semi-silent secular deity, old Roly — always with me. Driving me home is part of what he does. He knows how 'driving the drunk home' works. You don't need Roly. You actually turned down having a car and driver. You're a brave and sober grown-up. You can drive yerself home. Drive carefully, Nica."

The *Cimarron* inmate with whom I wanted to be nakedly body-to-body was Danny Wechsler.

Tall, baldingly blond, funny and smart as hell, Danny was writer, director, ringmaster, nurse and warden (as required) for all the *Cimarron* inmates.

Early in the run, after avoiding personal acknowledgement for a while, we had a long and lovely dinner at *La Giaconda,* a Malibu-modern seacoast restaurant, and Danny told me his Texas/Jewish/Danish history.

He was born and raised in the Texas town of Falfurrias ("pronounced 'foul furious', and if you were a tall blond Jewish kid, it was both of those things"). His mother was half Danish, which was why he frequently greeted me on set with "Good Morning, my fellow Scandinavian." His Mum's other half was German-Jewish. His father, Abraham Wechsler, was fully Austrian-Jewish. In the small town, the Wechslers were one of two Jewish families, as in "Billy Jim, would'ja run down to the Jew's an' get some milk an' donuts."

Danny's "Abie in Texas" grocer father had a heavy Austrian-Jewish accent and inspired *Cimarron's* Doctor Hacking Koffman.

Tall, blond and pug-nosed, young Danny sometimes tried telling his schoolmates he was a Danish boy who'd been adopted by the Wechslers. Falfurrias was too small a place for that story to be believed — too many people knew exactly when and where he was born.

So, as with many of us who do not mix well with childhood peers, he discovered the sanctuary of film. In Falfurrias, these were called "Moo'm Pitchers," "pitchers," or "the show." Seeing the show, a double feature with a cartoon, at the Alhambra cost very little.

The Alhambra became Danny's temple. He worshipped there and read all he could about film and filmmakers. It turned out that many of the best filmmakers in America were Jews. Like his father. Like half his mother. Like three fourths of his tall blond self.

Armed with this knowledge, he started making short documentary and fiction films while still in High School. Then he sent some films and an application to the University of California at Los Angeles. He was accepted. At UCLA, he won a few international University film awards, joined a union and became an assistant director in television. He then, with much tabloid attention, became director of *Kitty and the Connollys*, an award-winning show, when the show's star and executive producer said that Danny was the only person she would allow to direct her. He also persuaded the star that their sleeping together would "screw up the show" (though he knew the rules and slept with her twice — once to prove he thought she was attractive, the second time because women who want to sleep with you find only once insulting).

Kitty and the Connollys (with awards for Danny) led to *The Laird of Venice Beach* and his first work — partnering with Mari and Iain Mac Innis, the "mad Scottish geniuses" who created *The Laird of V.B.* That show begat a brief first marriage that ended in amicable indifference and legal formality, and a re-teaming with the Mac Innises for *Cimarron;* all of which had given Danny Wechsler almost two decades of award-larded job security.

By the time we got to Malibu coffee and brandy, Danny had completed his history, leaving us both with nothing but shared desire, and self-conscious as hell. More shy than I'd ever seen him (not unlike my father when he explained the miracle of menstruation to the ten-year-old me), he finally said barely audibly, "I think, Nica, that we … want the same thing. And that it matters. I also think that our … following that path … would … jostle Gareth."

"Yes … I know."

We agreed that Gareth was the glue that held *Cimarron* together ("You've heard of Crazy Glue?"), and that I was the glue that held Gareth together.

"I, we, don't dare fool with that, Nica. Pull out one piece of this puzzle, the central piece, and we'll wind up with a pile of funny disconnected shapes. … I really do hope we, you and I, can have our time. I know we're supposed to."

"Me too."

We paid the bill, walked into the sea air and snogged like teenagers in the La Giaconda parking lot — and again under a tree in Topanga Canyon. All breathless giggles and flesh-ache, we managed to stop short of what we both understood as completion.

The following day on the *Cimarron* set, we were sleepy, self-conscious and shy, but only for that one day. The Malibu night was never mentioned while I was part of *Cimarron.* It was also good that Gareth, who saw everything (for as long as he could see *anything*), was not on set that day.

The third and fourth time I renewed my *Cimarron* contract, I built in a proviso that allowed me to do a European or an American feature film during the summer hiatus. This proviso guaranteed that I would have a minimum of two months in which to film said feature.

I made this request primarily because, after two years, and despite excellent scripts and colleagues, I needed desperately to play somebody other than Lili Dangereuse.

The Americans were not interested in anything but variations of Lili.

The French, the Italians and the Swedes, bless them, were interested in Nica Lind, the actress. I did films in all three countries, one per country. Two of them did well. The one with the weak script and crazy director (Italian script, Romanian director) did badly. On balance, my European career remained a living thing. As a bonus, my father was cinematographer on the Swedish film, a period piece about the Danish tyrant, Valdemar Atterdag, shot in Visby, on the Baltic Swedish Island of Gotland.

My heart was at home, my work vitalised, and my European career bolstered.

My father, as always with me, was wise.

After filming finished, I stayed a week with Papa at his ancient flat in Stockholm's Old Town. He was at me daily about "making sure you always return home," saying that all I had built in Europe would die if I did not keep supporting it, and, "You will be left in Hollywood — a living telecartoon with … a diminutive … rake."

"It's 'rack', Papa."

Telecartoon or no, I would soon be a thirty-eight-year-old foreign actress in Hollywood.

My almost ten years in L.A. had taught me the age-rules for women in American film:

Birth to one year old — baby

One to two years old — unemployable

Two to 3 years old — toddler

3-7 years old — child

7-10 years old — older child and sometime partygoer. Cosmetic dentistry.

10-13 — pre-teen and more frequent partygoer. Late cosmetic dentistry.

13-17 — teenager and raving partygoer or studious loner. Possibly gay, possible cosmetic surgery.

17-19 — older teenager. Raving partygoer or studious loner. Possible parent. Possibly gay. Possibly married. Cosmetic surgery.

19-25 — young adult, possible rehab, possible parent. Possibly married. Possibly gay. Possible divorce.

25-30 — older young person. Loses work to younger young
people.
30-40 — semi-old. Play Doctors, lawyers and mothers.
More television work than big screen.
40-50 — old person but not old enough to play old people.
Too cute to be old; too old to be cute. Not young enough
to be sexy (without major surgeries). Not dead but might
as well be. Expected to play roles of women who are …
50-60 — most of whom have had too much cosmetic surgery and
have become real estate agents who act occasionally
(which is remarkable, as they are widely considered dead).
70-Death — character actor. Plays very old people.
At 38, I was about to segue from Semi-Old to Old Person.

Philip Rosenthal sent flowers, champagne and hand-written cards pleading with "Dearest Nica," his tiny-uddered cash cow, to reconsider and sign up for another three years of *Cimarron*.

Afraid that the seduction of being obscenely rich would sentence me to a three more years of "ooh la la," "Mais non, chéri," and "zut alors," interspersed with just enough episodes about love, loss, medical crisis and childhood horror to keep an actor from being taken, babbling, to a round rubber room, I went immediately to a lawyer who sent a thoughtful, gracious and notarised letter to Rosenthal at PRA and to the *Cimarron* producers. I also spent all day and most of a Sunday night writing personal notes of grateful thanks to every member of the cast and crew. Each of these notes was then courier-delivered, along with a bottle of outrageously expensive French wine (in one of its best years).

When the deed was done, definitely done, with no turning back, I threw a catered party at the Santa Monica poolhouse I was still rent-ing (my home, after all, was in Europe). The entire cast and crew of *You Mean This **Isn't** Cimarron?* filled the flat and huge deck. I also invited my landlord, Karl Freund, who offered the use of his Olympic-sized pool and spent the evening sipping champagne, singing his famous songs in a high, parched voice and regaling all the Pretty Little

Chickadees (and more than a few male film-buffs) with tales of Weimar, G.W. Pabst, Leni Riefenstahl, and Josef von Sternberg.

Augie Particelli attended, bringing his two daughters, who, being under ten years old and almost as large as their father, had undefined racks.

Philip Cuffs Rosenthal did not attend. He was furious with me and told Mari and Iain (who were producers as well as writers of *Cimarron*) that I was "another self-deluded one-show wonder. And a foreigner. In two years she'll be unhireable here, except as nostalgia."

Cuffs wasn't wrong. In America, I was a One-Show-Wonder. In Europe, I had a career, a family, a life.

People were having a good time at my party. I went upstairs to start packing. Not because I didn't have a week to pack — I just felt like affirming my choice.

Gareth Willett was asleep in my bed, fully dressed in his usual black jeans and black cotton turtleneck sweater. Thoughtfully, he had somehow managed to stay upright long enough to remove his black motorcycle boots before collapsing. The hair product that punk-spiked his black-and-grey hair was going to leave a grease patch on my pillowcase. Oh well, I thought, there are many pillowcases but only one Gareth.

I knew there was no coy ploy in his being in my bed; the alcohol to skin-container ratio had simply tipped, as it did every day, and it was past his awake-time.

I sat on the white rattan chest at the foot of the bed looking at a face that was so matinee-idol perfect that even massive dissipation could not leech the star quality from it. The Barrymore nose, the full lower lip, the tangle of black eyelashes and comic-book hero's jaw — all this and the prodigious talent that even occupation-based self-loathing could not kill — filled me with a tender understanding of imminent loss. My eyes filled and I rested my hand on his chest, whispering, "Goodbye for now, Loup Garou."

He opened his chocolate-brown eyes.

"What, Frenchy? What did you say?"

"I said 'Goodbye for now, Loup Garou'."

He moaned, afraid to move his head, and took a deep breath.

"Right. Always wanted to ask. Was afraid to. Afraid it might be a bad thing. Who's this Garoo bloke when he's at home?"

"Loup Garou. He's a French mythical monster. A handsome werewolf … who can transform himself into anything on a full moon night. You are a Loup Garou, *my* Loup Garou, who can transform himself at *any* time."

He smiled goofily, not fully in control of his lips.

"Sound's right. … I do …" The energy burst could not sustain. He closed his eyes again, breathing heavily but steadily.

I held both my hands over my mouth to keep from sobbing. Tears rolled out of my eyes and over my hands. I wiped face with hands and hands on bedcover. Then I stood up and left the room, closing the door behind me.

On the landing, I leaned against the white wooden railing, watching my carousing colleagues on the floor below. I didn't hear Danny Wechsler approach.

"Good evening, my fellow Scandinavian."

My fellow-Scandinavian and I watched the crowd for a while. I felt he should be the first to speak, and knew, in general, what he would say.

"Well, Miss Nica. Now that you're not doing the show … could we … go out?"

I looked him fully in the Danish blue eyes.

"I'm leaving for Europe next week."

"You're here until … never mind. I see your point. I don't want to … be … hurriedly … with you on your way to the airport."

Both of us were running on held inbreath.

I exhaled and put my hand on the railing, over his hand.

"Écoute, mon Danny. I know we should have our time. Our completion. Life is crazy. It sends us all over the place. I do not know what will happen, but I hope …"

"Me too, Nica. Very much."

I exhaled again, a slow outbreath.

"We should join the party."

"Yes."

We headed down the stairs; first me, all bubbly polyglot and laughter, and, five minutes later, Danny.

10 Paris, Mon Pays, et Maman

LES TOITS DE PARIS. The orange roofs of Paris as seen from the air. Home.

I'd arranged to have my pack-rat L.A. acquisitions, including boxes of press-clippings, pictures and legal documents, sent to the large (and therefore undercluttered) flat I'd recently bought for my father in Östermalm Square in Stockholm.

So I only had a mid-sized tiny-wheeled push-bag and an oversized turquoise parachute silk handbag when I arrived, in the pearlised Parisian drizzle, at our family flat in Montparnasse.

Maman was standing on our shallow iron-railed balcony, waving at me and shouting, "Bienvenue, Dominique, bienvenue!"

The taxi driver, who had been kind enough to recognise "Madame Nica Lind," also recognised "Madame Laure Normand" and joined me in waving up at the balcony. "Salut, Madame Normand," he shouted. "Je vous admire beaucoup!"

"Merci, Monsieur!" Maman shouted in reply.

The driver then said his wife also admired Maman, and me as well. Either he and his wife had no children or their children did not admire my mother and me. In any case, it was a lovely welcome home, but nowhere near as wonderful as taking the birdcage elevator to the fifth floor and being embraced by the familiar-from-birth smell and touch that was Maman.

She had written me, some months earlier, saying she was going to have "some tightening of my visage. For the camera." There also needed to be dentistry. Having piles of money and no time at all in which to spend it, I happily paid for all this.

Maman smiled, turned her face to the light.

"Well, my little Dominique, what do you think of your investment?"

Whoever did it had done well. Maman had lost some nuances of animation but she did not have that hospital bedsheets tightness. Her usually shoulder-length wavy hair was now a light brown with punky spiky white blonde streaks.

"You look beautiful, Maman. As always. I like the punk hair."

"It's fun. Something new. We do our best. And time does his worst. Come. You must be starving. I have some food from the charcuterie."

"No, Maman. I cannot. I never can sleep properly on overnight flights. If it would be all right, I would just like to go to my bed for a while."

Maman agreed that air travel was bad for proper sleep. I collected my bags and she walked me to my old room. At the oak door to the room, still with its ancient ceramic "Dominique" nametag and brass dolphin doorpull, she hugged me again, kissed me three times — cheek-cheek-cheek — and said she would wake me for dinner.

My room. White eyelet ceiling-to-floor curtains, a matching ruffle at the top. Black velvet theatre draperies at each corner, to be drawn in front of the white openwork when one wanted to shut out the light.

My little carved oak bed had been replaced by an adult-sized exact replica, with a carved squirrel at each of its four posts, each squirrel holding an acorn in its articulated forepaws ("I have replaced your old bed with a larger one of the same style," Maman had written, six years earlier). I touched the rounded squirrel-heads, feeling a bit like Garbo in *Queen Christina*.

On the new version of the old bed, atop the cluster of needlepoint pillows I'd collected in adolescence, rested my old friend Babar the Elephant.

I gently placed pillows and Babar on the carved Chinese chest that lived in front of my bed. I then pulled off white running shoes, yellow nubby socks, faded jeans and snug yellow shirt. Too tired to wash, I wiped at lipstick and makeup with a tissue from the plastic holder on the bed-table.

After drawing velvet darkness over white curtains, I threw back the white duvet and sheet, climbed into bed and pulled the cool coverings over my naked body. I awoke when Maman knocked gently and then opened the door.

Thanks to the velvet drapes, it was almost pitch dark. Maman was carrying a white wicker breakfast tray, which she placed on a small round table. On this tray were two croissants, jam, a small creamer filled with hot milk, and a cafetière of black coffee.

She pulled back the draperies, revealing a sunny morning. "Bonjour," she said.

"Bon *jour?* It was supposed to be 'bon *soir'!* Have I slept for a day and a night?" I sat up in bed, pulling pillows behind my head.

Maman laughed.

"Yes, Dominique. And I believe this is just and proper. You have been doing the same film, day and night, for eight years!"

The telephone rang. It was my father, calling from Stockholm.

"Hello Papa. It is wonderful to hear your voice. And to know that we are on the same side of the ocean."

"Well, Nica, I don't know. I've got all these boxes of your belongings but your mother gets you. Is that how it works?"

Papa had known I was going first to Paris. His teasing question was just Papa-speak for hello. I could hear through the phone-line how happy he was that I was back in Europe. And knew he could hear my happiness meeting his own.

We nattered for about half an hour, Maman having gone to her room to change for dinner, which we would be having at a favourite bistrot in the Rue du Cherche Midi.

I assured Papa that I had my ongoing air-ticket for Stockholm and would be arriving, as planned, in four days.

"And you will help me unpack these boxes, yes? I am an old man now, you know."

"Please do not touch those boxes. I will deal with all of them when I arrive."

"Well, perhaps the day *after* you arrive. We should first just visit, I think. And I'm glad you will sort them. When they arrived I thought I would have to sleep in the street with the drunk, the crazy lady and the man who plays the banjo."

"Now, Papa. You said I should send the boxes to you. You said your new flat was very big."

"Yes. Very big and filled with light. I've worked all my life with light but never lived with it. It's good. I'm still getting used to it but it is very good indeed."

We acknowledged that we loved each other, in Swedish, French and English. Suddenly overwhelmed by my good fortune, I poured a sherry from a sideboard bottle and, as happens to me with one quick drink, it simultaneously warmed my belly and stopped the incipient tears.

11 Carignac

MAMAN AND I WENT to see Jean Marie Carignac.

In his nineties and very ill, Carignac was living in a palliative care home just outside of Paris.

His room was airy and sunny. A simple white table was filled with flowers, photos and cards. He was propped up in the middle of his single steel-sided bed like a tiny wizened marionette. Even from the door of the room I saw that his eyes were covered with a thin film, not unlike the petroleum jelly camera operators put on lenses years ago to soften the focus.

"Salut, my Jean Marie," Maman said.

Carignac knew her voice instantly. "Laure!" he croaked. The Carignac voice, always raspy, broken by too many cigarettes for too many years, was almost gone.

He grinned as widely as he could, though the Shar-Pei folds of his face no longer expanded when he smiled, but lay in thick, soft yellow-white strips. Much of his corporeal self had withered, but his will to joy was unmistakable and would not be gone until Carignac was gone.

Which, we'd been told, would be very soon. His tiny body was so irretrievably riddled with cancers that he'd asked for "only the sweet pills, the ones that ease pain and make me float."

Maman told him I was with her. He patted the edges of the bed for us to sit, which we did, one on each side of our fragile friend.

"Salut, Maître," I said, not sure I could say much more.

"Dominique is back from America, my Jean Marie. You are the only person she asked to see. She has been away a long while, or …"

"Or I would have been here to see you sooner. I am so glad to see you! I have ... a very fine work life, and it all started with you. With my parents and with you!"

Tears began to run in rivulets through the crevasses of his face.

"No, no. Please don't cry. You have brought so much joy. Please forgive me if I made you cry. I love you. All the film-makers in Paris, in Europe, love you."

And that made him cry more. Maman looked at me as if I were hopeless. So I told three dirty jokes in French and, mercifully, Carignac laughed, making small gurgly sounds.

I asked if I could hug him. He said he would like that, but that I would have to do it very gently, like the "ladies of the bath."

I embraced him, barely touching, as if he were made of the thinnest glass. He rested his head on my shoulder. He smelled like old paper, baby oil, urine and tobacco. He said I smelled like cinnamon. I said, "And you smell like ... like the *Cinéma de la Cinémathèque de Montmartre.*"

His head still resting on my shoulder, he spoke, barely audibly, into my neck.

"Like ... my ... Cinémathèque. ... This ... pleases ... me."

Two nurses entered the room. They said it was time for M. Carignac to rest. Maman and I stood, Maman leaning forward and brushing Carignac's lips with her own. She promised to return "in the next days." I leaned down and also kissed him lightly, knowing I would not see him alive again.

In the taxi from Seine et Oise to Paris, Maman and I held hands, looked down into our laps and did not say a word.

12 Stockholm, Papa

TWO DAYS LATER I WAS IN SWEDEN, at Årlanda Airport.

Papa, never one for waving or shouting, stood patiently, holding his ancient grey-brown fedora in his hands, waiting for me to pick him out of the crowd. We embraced and headed for the luggage carousel.

Stockholm, famous for cold winters and night that comes in mid-afternoon, does the best summer in Europe. Sunny, clear and without the thick humidity that oppresses so many places.

Papa's new flat was in the large square of one of Stockholm's more posh neighbourhoods.

"Strange for an old cameraman from Södermalm and Gamla Stan to be living with all these rich people, all these embassies, all these old ones. Of the three, we have only 'old' in common. But it is peaceful. Old Swedes are good about peaceful. Even young Swedes do not rush about screaming in the street very much. We old Swedes appreciate this. I've not been in California for at least fifteen years. I see pictures on the television news of young Californians running about and screaming. Young *and* old. Old Californians can be very young. Do Californians run through the streets and scream all the time now?"

I laughed and told him that Californians drove everywhere in cars. They did not run through the streets at all, really. "Even if you are dating someone, you go everywhere in your two cars." Papa nodded and said I was right, said he'd forgotten. Said it had been that way when he was there. "Cars. Always cars."

Papa's building was five stories high, cream white and quite wide. There were two alabaster gargoyles framing the outside door. I took my gear from the back seat of Papa's ancient navy blue Volvo and we rode the elevator to the second floor ("Sometimes the elevator dies, but it is not many stairs to walk. Even an old man like me can do it").

I noted that Papa was using the word "old" rather a lot in reference to himself. Having just seen the little broken doll that had been Jean Marie Carignac, the thought made me shiver so I pushed it away.

His flat was huge. My 30 large boxes, mostly books, clothing and CDs, plus five carefully crated paintings and a small sculpture, took up one side of the large living room. Bits of furniture were scattered here and there, including a tattered old sofa and a fine blue velvet antique chair with thick carved snakes for arms. We have to go furniture shopping, I thought.

Papa had recreated his Paris study, only with far more space. There were thousands of books, cans of film, CDs and DVDs. "I'm converting almost everything to digital. I've so very much film. It takes time. Some of it is too faded to convert. Did you know, Nica, that I have shot three hundred and seventy-five films?! And that does not count the television ones. Nobody can say that Bo Lindskog did not work for his living!"

We sautéed diced chicken breast, vegetables and rice in a spicy butter-sauce. I made a salad of tomatoes and arugula. There was fine French white wine to celebrate my arrival, but he'd not yet bought furniture for the dining room, so we ate at the large kitchen table, which over-looked a verdant and multi-flowered summer garden.

We sat on the old living room sofa, waiting for night to fully come. When it did, and Östermalm Square was illuminated by tall wrought iron streetlamps, we returned to the kitchen for our dinner.

Always loving to play with light, he'd lit three fat white candles, which were in small plates on the table. Other candles were flickering on the countertop or, with protective glass over them, on the kitchen wall.

I looked at my father's face in the candlelight. It was, as always, a long thin face, grave and monastic in repose, young and mischievous when he smiled. He did not look old or young. He never had looked either. Not to me. He had one of those Medieval-carving faces. Ageless and aged all at once.

Of course, I realised with some surprise, I had never seen my father as a young man, apart from photos. Typically of those who photograph others, he did not have many photos of himself. A few as an only-child boy. A few as a young man. Some with colleagues or clipped from film magazines. Seven or eight with Maman and me. Actors, I thought, have so many pictures of themselves.

When Papa and Maman married, he was already 49. I studied the face of my father. Could he now be eighty, I wondered? He did not look eighty. Or 49. He looked, with slightly thinner, whiter hair, like Papa.

"I see your wheels turning, Nica. What are you thinking?"

"I was thinking about age. Today, you have used the word 'old' a number of times, in reference to yourself. Do you feel old?"

He smiled. "Ach," he said, "sometimes I do. But that is only because I am old. Most of the time I go about my business and do not think about it. But my bones hurt sometimes. Osteo-arthritis. I take pills and supplements for this but my fingers are stiffer. So are my legs. I walk every morning and I'm doing this Chinese Tai Chi business. There's a place across the square where one can do this. Sometimes we do it in the square. Mostly old — excuse me — not young people. It is lovely, the Tai Chi. There is one very pretty young woman, about your age, who does it also. You could do it with me if you wish. Some time."

Papa reached across the table and put his long-fingered hand over mine. His hand did not look stiff. It looked as it always had — Rodin beautiful.

The following day, I heard Papa leaving the flat very early in the morning. I went to my window and looked out and down to the huge Östermalm Square. In the centre of the square was a group of people in loose, mostly grey or white sweatshirts, tee shirts and Yoga pants. My father joined them, seamlessly entering into the gentle but highly focused repetitive movements of Tai Chi.

As Papa had said, it was mostly greyheads. And one young woman, in a coral tanktop, ballet slippers and baggy white cotton pants, her long blonde hair plaited into a loose braid that hung down her back.

She was tall and slim; a body very much like my own. She was also, even from the distance of our window, obviously about twenty-one years old. I smiled. Daughters are ever-young to their fathers.

For over six months I wandered about in Stockholm, mostly with Papa.

I unpacked boxes and set up my room, which had the same garden view as the kitchen. Papa and I reminisced when I showed him my tiny sculpture — a bronze of Marlene Dietrich as Lola in *The Blue Angel*.

We bought furniture, ate in restaurants, cooked for each other, saw films and plays. We travelled around Sweden and attended film festivals where we were celebrated in a warm but unfussy Swedish way.

I persuaded Papa to accompany me to an art auction in a Gamla Stan gallery. My frugal father discovered that he quite liked bidding on things and had the winning bid on two paintings: one nude of a young Greek or Italian looking girl, and one painting of the actual street where he was born in Södermalm, a now trendy but once only working-class Stockholm neighbourhood.

"You know," he said when we got back to the flat, as he hung his new paintings, "Garbo was also born in Söder. Gustafsson was her name. Greta Gustafsson."

He was concerned about my spending.

"Look," I told him, "for almost ten years I made ridiculous amounts of money, because the American television people were willing to let me do that. But I also worked damn near day and night, so there was no way to spend any of it, except in paying large taxes, which I paid, or in giving it to people and things that mattered — AIDS in the arts, AIDS in Africa, juvenile literacy, single mothers, film scholarships — which I did. This giving helped with the taxes but it also made me feel less like a slut for taking so much money.

"They really do make it hard to spend the money. When you go to award shows, or any other high visibility situation, the best designers give you free clothing and the jewellers lend you jewellery. I did not want most of the jewellery, so I didn't buy it. Even if I did want a piece of jewellery, it's always accompanied by armed men and requires insane amounts of insurance. Everyone in L.A. buys houses, but I don't want a house in L.A. That's how they trap you — you create your dream house and then feel you must live in it. Or trade it for another house and live there.

"Listen, Papa, until after I was graduated from film and theatre school in London, you and Maman paid for every single thing I needed or wanted. Now, for a while, I can buy things for you both, *and* for me. Apart from this flat for you and the place I'm buying Maman in Nice, I have not been very extravagant. Hell, I'm still living with my parents! And I *will* go back to work soon. I'm just having a holiday. And buying things for two people I love, who have always earned their own money. Understood?"

My father nodded. He then asked me to have an akavit with him. "To film," he toasted, "and to the Americans, who were crazy enough to give my fine daughter ridiculous amounts of money."

In early January, I came home in the afternoon night, carrying bags of clothing from the Stockholm shops — the best winter sales in Europe.

Papa came out of his study, script in hand.

"Are you ready to go back to work? I'm going, with you or without you. They want us both."

"Who?"

"The Americans."

"I don't want to go to America now."

"You don't have to. They are filming in Helsingfors."

"Finland?"

"Yes, my Nica, *that* Helsingfors."

13 Lind and Lindskog Go to Finland

PAPA SAID IT WAS A GOOD ROLE in a good script. A Russian reuniting with his father and half-sister in Finland. The male star would be Nick Balanov, a very good Russian-American actor who'd recently won major awards for playing a blind Russian Gypsy singer in Paris in the 1920s. "Apparently, Balanov is in love with a French actress — that does happen to men — and he was looking for a film that would keep him in Europe. You, Nica, would play the half-sister. Half-Russian, half Finnish-Swede. You and your half-brother fall in love. Here. Read. I think you'll like it. And you know the cinematographer. A talented old Swede, I'm told."

The talented old Swede handed me the script.

"Here. Read. They need to know by Friday. You are their first choice for the role."

"It's an American film. My American agent fired me when I left *Cimarron*."

"I'm your agent for this. They called me about both of us."

"Do I pay you a commission?"

"You have. We're living in it. Go read."

I headed down the hall to my room, turning for a moment to ask one more question.

"Papa, who's directing?"

"Danny Wechsler, your director from *Cimarron*. It was he who asked for you."

Papa and I took the famous "Dricka Boat" (Drunk Boat) from Sweden to Finland.

This was an enormous ferry, complete with staterooms, casino, slot machines, restaurant, all-night buffet, three or four bars, vast duty-free shop, Karaoke lounge, and ubiquitous slot machines.

The ferry was called "drunk boat" because it travelled overnight and free beer taps were everywhere and unwatched. One could also buy all sorts of alcohol very cheaply, in the duty-free. As a result of this constant booze flow, most passengers were at least half-pissed when they arrived at their destination. Women of all ages were frequently advised to stay in or near their staterooms after nine in the evening. Some men, travelling in groups of three or four, would leave their stateroom doors open and shout invitations in various languages. "Hello chickie, come and have a drink with four rich businessmen from Linköping!" was one of my favourites.

Papa and I ate early at the buffet, while there was reasonable sobriety. Except for the little bespectacled blond boy who, after cranking draft lager three or four times, was trying to determine the flavour of a large tub of ice cream and fell head first into the orange goo. He was rescued, his rescuers laughing as they cleaned his face and spectacles with serviettes.

After dining on all sorts of wonderful fish and side dishes, plus an akavit and lager, Papa and I headed back to our staterooms, stopping briefly to play slot machines. My father, the newborn auction bidder, also quite liked it when coins noisily filled the well.

There was a Karaoke stage behind us. A young woman was singing "Strangers in the Night" without a trace of melody. Finally, the extraordinary dissonance started to break my brains and I told Papa I'd go to my stateroom.

"No, no, Nica. I want to walk you there. It is too crazy for you to go alone."

As we headed through the lounge to our stateroom corridor, we saw a young Romany couple sitting at a small table. The young woman was enormous — perhaps the largest woman I'd ever seen, and exquisitely beautiful. She had what Papa would call "her own key light." A face that seemed illuminated from within. All the features were in perfect proportion. Huge brown eyes, full lips, straight nose, strong chin.

Her companion, a handsome young man of about her age and half her size, had his hands under her floor-length traditional Roma black velvet dress. As his hands climbed higher, massaging as they travelled, she closed her huge eyes, wet her lips, moaned and laughed. The flat silvery metal coins that ringed her dress at mid hip jingled as we passed them.

"What an extraordinary face she has," said my father the Cameraman.

"That also," I replied.

At nine in the morning we disembarked, amongst inebriates, businessmen laden with bags of booze, women laden with duty-free scarves, gloves and cosmetics, teenaged ski-trippers, bleary-eyed children, and three tiny Russian pole dancers with long hair-extension pony tails and bright red fingernails.

The Romany couple was in the terminal building when Papa and I got there. The huge beautiful young woman was standing in the middle of the room. Her hands had swept up thick masses of shiny titian hair. Her eyes were closed, her Ingrid Bergman lips open in a smile, revealing large perfect teeth that were born not made.

Three buttons of her velvet dress, between the navel and thighs, had been opened. Her lover, on his knees in front of her, had his face inside the opening. The epic goddess undulated and moaned.

No one in the terminal looked at the pair. Three ruddy-faced young skiers, two girls and a boy, walked around them, chatting, committed to seeing nothing as they headed out of the terminal with purposeful athleticism. Others did the same.

My father and I were waiting to be collected by someone from the film company. Papa's adjustment to the cunnilingual display was to read his script and make notes. I tried to do the same. At one point though, my gaze pulled upward to the activity in the centre of the terminal. The woman looked at me, past the bodies moving quickly, carefully and not too close to her, to the outside of the building.

"You have a problem with this," her eyes asked, with a not inconsiderable angry power.

No, no, I sent back as strongly as I could, nodding slightly, politely — no problem at all. I returned my eyes to the script and kept them there, seeing nothing.

Helsinki, Finland in February is colder than Stockholm, Sweden in February (and Stockholm in February is certainly cold enough). In layers of clothing, only my eyes showing, I waddled from my hotel down the wide expanse of Esplanadi, one of the two grand ceremonial roads in the centre of the city, script and thermos of mint tea in a canvas bag, the bag's handle in my thinsulate-gloved hand.

The first read-through of *Finlandia* would take place in a large room on the upper floor of a popular and expensive art nouveau (or "Jugendstil," as the Finns called the period, using the German word) restaurant. To add to the linguistic polyglot, the restaurant had a French name — *La Tulipe*.

The room was laid out in the traditional fashion for first readings: a huge rectangular table and chairs with pencils, blank paper and maps in the centre. Blue pages of schedule stacked neatly in alongside the pencils. The producers and production team were standing, waiting to greet the actors, of which I was, as ever, the first to arrive. And the only face I really saw was Danny Wechsler's.

"Hello, my fellow Scandinavian. Welcome to Finland."

"Hello, Nica. Very glad you've signed on."

"Me too."

Danny looked over his shoulder at a slim blonde woman. She looked a bit like me. Only younger. Twenty-something. Danny waved her over. She approached shyly.

"Nica, this is my wife Carolee."

Actors are trained in quick recovery. You'd have to run that moment in slo-mo to see my head twitch, my eyes widen.

"Hello, Carolee. Pleasure to meet you. And congratulations to you both. When did you marry?"

"Three months ago. We'd been talking about it for a while. Then one day Danny flat-out proposed and I said yes. I loved him from when we first met."

"And when was that … if it's not too personal."

"No, it's fine. We met five years ago. Danny had some legal business with my boss, Greg Van Ness, the real estate lawyer. One thing led to another and we started dating. It was hard, because of Danny's work schedule. But you know about that."

"Yes. I know about that. It's wonderful to have some time for myself again. And time to do fine films. Are you going to be working with us, Carolee?"

She giggled. "Gosh, no. I don't know anything about film-making. And we're going to have a baby. I'll be going back to L.A. in a few days to hold the fort at home. I wish you all the best with the picture."

My father had chosen his seat, off to one side of the table. He'd set up pencils, paper and script. He poured coffee from his thermos. He was watching me. Danny, Carolee and me. I don't know what he knew about what he was watching. Being my father, he probably knew everything. And being my father, he would not say anything about any of it unless I did.

Nick Balanov entered the room. Danny introduced him to me. We each said it was a pleasure. We each said we admired the other's work. We each meant it.

People were filing in. Sherm Field, the American producer, short, compact, well tailored, greeted everyone. His assistant, Durrie Cole, directed us to where we should sit for the read-through. Timo Halonen, our Finnish co-producer, tall, with red-brown longish hair, a short beard, bushy moustache, a big smile and a red-brown version of the Frida Kahlo eyebrow, welcomed us all to his country as cast and crew contact sheets were distributed.

"My home and mobile numbers are there, if anyone needs me. Durrie Cole and my assistant Anne Lappalainen can also be contacted by phone and mobile. Your hotel, The Grand Boulevardi, can also help with anything you need to know. I am very pleased to have such a fine cast, director, cinematographer and crew. Again, welcome to Helsinki/Helsingförs. We are going to tell a wonderful story together. Thank you all."

Durrie asked if any of us wanted to use the toilet before we started to read. I raised my hand and was excused.

It was a bank of four single unisex toilets. I entered one, locked the door, said all sorts of mean-spirited angry things about Danny Wechsler and his cute peppy "Oh Gosh" wife, finally acknowledging that the man had a right to a life and a wife and a family. I washed my hands, freshened my lipstick and headed back to the read-through. Which was first-rate and fully focused. We were all very well-cast and Gunnar Tikkanen, who was playing the father to Nick Balanov and me, was, we could all see even in the bare bones of first-read, superb.

I was packing everything in the canvas bag when Danny approached.

"Nica ... you read wonderfully. As you know, you were my first choice for this role. Thank you so much."

"You can stop thanking me, Danny. I loved the script. And love working with the director. Who has a right to marry."

"When we spoke at your place ... Carolee and I had separated. I'm not a "Hollywood player," Nica. Never have been. There was a strong chemistry, something special between you and me. Then Carolee was pregnant. So we married. And I do love her. I have for some time."

"Good. Fine. Not a problem. I wish you both a happy and healthy life. And now I must catch up with my father, who is waiting for me downstairs in the restaurant. We need to eat early and I need to look at my lines and sleep early. See you on the set. Goodnight."

We, the actors, *were* very well-cast, and filming, as it does at its best, took on a life of its own. Our hydra-headed creature, the animal called *Finlandia,* was a strong and healthy beast. When Nick Balanov and I worked through what was called "the incest scene," the crew applauded — always a good sign. Unless the crew was applauding because it was freezing bloody cold and they were glad the long night-shoot was finally over.

My father, who loved shooting hand-held "wild shots" with an old Arriflex camera, could no longer carry the heavy Arri. Pelle, his young Swedish assistant, carried it, as Papa tramped through the snow beside him, wheeling and swooping in imitation of what he wanted Pelle to shoot.

The Finns are not as obsessive as the Swedes about snow removal, and once one left the centre of town there were moon-surface ice lumps everywhere. Most of us used ski poles to walk about in the ice-lump zones. Or fell down a lot.

Danny and I worked well, with a long-known shared language. When we were not filming, I avoided his company, choosing instead to dine with my father or with Nick Balanov and Gunnar Tikkanen, who lived in the countryside with one wife and ten dogs. Gunnar had pictures of these dogs and stories about each of them.

Papa remained discreetly unquestioning about the "something" between his daughter and her director.

When we finished the final scene, Nick and I walking through the snow with our father walking slowly behind us, the sound man called for Room Tone and we all stood still. Then we walked in the snow, without speaking. "That's a wrap!" the assistant director shouted in English, Swedish and Finnish. We all clomped off to the warm "holding room," where there was applause, beer and akavit. Most of us hugged. I hugged Danny, saying, "A pleasure, as always. See you at the premiere," and then moved quickly to my dressing trailer.

I was packing up when there was a knock. It was Nick Balanov.

"Nica? Can I ask a favour?"

"Sure Nick, what do you need?"

"A date. A totally platonic date."

It was a bit more complicated than that.

Nick had been invited to an orgy — what he called "a scene," in a private home in the chic Embassy district.

"I've never been to one. Never really thought about it. Would like to see what it's about, at least once. I've been assured that it's discreet and very private and we don't have to do anything, we can just have a drink, look around and leave …"

"We?"

"That's the thing. I feel shy about going alone. I know that's goofy, but there it is. I'm a Midwestern Russian-American farm boy who's been invited to his first and probably last orgy. If you could just walk me in and hang out for a half hour, you could split and I'll stay if I want to, or split with you."

Whatever I was expecting anyone to say to me on this shoot, this was none of it. I rubbed my hand over my eyes.

"Nick. I'm having dinner with my father, who is waiting for me at *La Tulipe*. What do I tell him? 'Sorry, I can't have dinner with you Papa. I'm going to an orgy with Nick Balanov'?"

"I'm sorry. I shouldn't bother you with this. It's just that I've never been to an orgy …"

"And I've never killed anyone. But I don't have to do it to know I don't want to."

"You *have* killed people. All actors have. On stage. In film. We've explored it. That's why most actors don't kill people. I've never been to an orgy. And I've never acted in one."

"Interesting theory. Very homeopathic. Actors inoculate themselves by having a bit of the poison."

"It may not be poison. It may be fun. They will have big bowls of condoms."

"Big bowls of condoms. That's certainly *my* idea of a good time."

Nick blushed. A sweet and gifted man, with that always-surprising American innocence.

"All right, Nick. I'll walk you into your orgy. And once you are set-tled, I'll go home. Okay?"

"Great! Thanks, thanks a million Neeks."

"Don't call me 'Neeks', or the deal's off."

I rang my father at *La Tulipe*. Told him that Nick had asked me to dine
with two American friends. Papa said I should have a good time, that
he would see me tomorrow to go to the ferry terminal.

"Don't stay out too late, Nica. The ferry for Sweden goes at seven in
the morning."

As with all Embassy districts, there were security police and little
guardhouses in front of most buildings. They protected inhabitants from
invasions by thieves, vandals and others who wished them ill. I imag-
ined they also protected orgy-type events from police or paparazzi invasions. I hoped this assumption was correct.

The three-story Jugendstil mansion was beautiful — cream yellow
with a strip of white weaving through in waves and curlicues. The first-
floor windows were pre-Raphaelite women, created in leaded stained
glass.

We got out of the taxi, presented our invitation to the fox-coated door-
man and were quickly ushered inside. People, mostly male, were cir-
culating from room to room, taking glasses of champagne or red wine
from tray-carrying young women in abbreviated maids' uniforms.
Engelbert Humperdinck blared from wall speakers, celebrating Belsize
Bicycles.

"Well Nick, I'm ready to go now."

"You promised one half hour."

"Right. So I did."

There was a bar in the corner. I asked for an akavit. And then another.
I looked across the room. There stood The Pig Brothers. Manny and
Muni Oleisceivicz were twin Polish porn-makers who lived in Big Sur
California, behind electrified gates. Their films were, by porn standards,
not that gross. It was the Pig Brothers themselves who were gross.
Legendarily gross. Even worse than the stories about them were the PBs
themselves. Soft guts hung over their low-hanging khaki polyester
pants. They stank of sweat and cheap cologne that smelled like disinfectant.

Their yellow teeth smelled nasty also. Or so I'd been told by Gareth Willett, who had gone to one of their parties "to further demonstrate my total lack of self-respect." Without a word to Nick, I backed away from their line of vision and into another room. It was the cloak-room.

It being Finnish winter, the room was filled with coats, caps, scarves and boots. Precisely the sort of thing I was wearing.

"May I offer you a toga," inquired one of the handmaidens, holding out a basketful of yellow fabric.

To this day, I do not know why I said "yes please." Something about bravery. Something about curiosity. Something about Danny Wechsler. I will never know for sure.

Once I was in the tiny yellow silk toga that almost covered my buttock cheeks, Charybdis, who had joined Sister Scylla in the cloakroom, smilingly suggested that I would love it in the heated roof garden, "just up the stairs."

The stairs were even further away from the Pig Brothers, so, unable to see Nick anywhere, I took the advice and climbed the narrow spiral steps.

I opened the door to the clear plastic bubble-covered roof garden. It was a warm sanctuary from which I could see snowy and icy-cold Helsinki all about us. The huge bubble was ringed with tiny open portholes. Without these, I suspected we would all slow-cook in airless heat.

An attractive man pulled me to him, kissing me deeply and drawing me further into the bubble. There were potted plants everywhere, some of them tropical. There were bronze bowls of condoms everywhere. And there were bodies everywhere, doing what everywhere-bodies do at an orgy. I could see Nick on the other side of the bubble. He was standing. There were two slim young-looking men with him. One was kneeling in front of him. The other stood behind him, caressing his body and yanking at his hair. Nick's eyes were closed. He was smiling. I wondered if the "French actress" he loved in Paris was actually a man. The Americans, with their crazy closets, always required these double lives for their film stars. Everybody usually knew the truth. Late-night television comics made smirky winking jokes, but everyone did this bogus simultaneous hetero dance. It was good to be, once again, a European actor.

An actor and also a photographer's daughter, I wanted to watch, to study, but felt that would violate the unwritten etiquette of this sort of thing. And would not be possible. My kissing man, who had been stroking my body and nuzzling my neck, became two and then three. I was lowered onto an air mattress. People were all over me. They were surprisingly gentle, turning me this way and that, asking permission for this or that, respecting any "no."

At one point, someone asked if I liked girls. He laughed when I replied, "I like women as *people* but not for sex." I could hear this answer being repeated, could hear others laugh. The laughter, as with the crowded invasion of my body, was not mean-spirited. I felt myself thicken, glaze over and grow as large as a tall slim house. On my back, knees apart, propped up on my elbows, I looked about me. The people were full-sized but I felt like Gulliver, covered in Lilliputians, far above my enormous self, seeing us all. Little Lilliputians. Big Nica.

In the early years of film-making, my father had told me, they'd smear the camera lens with Vaseline to soften the focus. Years later, the Vaseline was replaced with diffusion lenses that could blur wrinkles and make soft even the harshest of faces. Orgies are gooey, I thought. They are pre-diffusion. I felt I was, along with the entire writhing, murmuring bubble-cluster, covered in Vaseline.

The blur sharpened and there before my eyes was Herb Gutnick.

Herb Gutnick was Gareth Willett's agent. For ten years he had asked to take me out. Not wishing to hurt his feelings, I always said I was "going with someone."

Herb Gutnick looked down at me, my naked body covered in humans.

"I suppose you're going with all these people," he said.

I quickly showered at the mansion, put my clothes on and called a taxi to take me to the Hotell Boulevardi.

In L.A. they have these "How Many" jokes (Question: How many Hollywood actors does it take to screw in a lightbulb? Answer: One to screw in the bulb, two to hold the ladder, and three more to ask, in unison, if their agent needs any other chores done before all six actors drive home, each in a separate used Honda). Riding to the Grand Hotell Boulevardi in the back of a Helsinki taxi, I knew how many people it took to equal nothing. At least one hundred. Possibly more.

In the lobby I rang Danny's room and asked to come up. "It's important. I won't take long."

"Of course, Nica. Come on up."

I told him what had happened. All of it, including the Polish Pig Brothers. I told him I knew he and I had passed our time. I told him that being immersed in a large group of naked people was intermittently sensual but completely not sexual for me. I told him I needed to complete my experience and could only do that as part of a twosome. I told him I wanted to complete my experience with him. That it would be a one-time thing and ...

Together, Danny Wechsler and I completed my experience. We also completed one of his. It was a one-time thing for as long as he was a loving husband and father.

Loving. There was a lot of love in our Finnish completion. Over ten years of love. There was holding and being held. There were the rocketing racketing explosions I'd loved since first discovering the repeated first-time that was the female orgasm — something I could not have in a naked crowd. There was trust and silly pun laughter ("So. 'Finnish' doesn't always have two 'n's'"). There was much joy.

And only hours of possible time. As I rested my head on Danny's chest, him stroking my hair, he said, "Oh Lordy, Nica. In L.A. we didn't do this because we only had a week. An' now we've got ...?"

"About another hour."

We showered and dressed. He escorted me to my room and kissed me sweetly.

"Goodbye, my fellow Scandinavian. Go safely, go well."

"You too, my Danny. Have a beautiful baby. See you at the premiere."

The Helsinki ferry terminal is a quiet place at six in the morning. No Romany lovers. No skiers. One stranger waiting at the far end of a long wooden bench behind me, with others to come. One ticket agent, half-asleep with nothing to do. On our bench, the first in a row of five, only my silent father and his silent daughter. In a corner, the soft wet sound of a doughy woman pushing a thick string mop into a bucket that smelled like the Pig Brothers, and then sloshing it around the floor. No past, no future. Only the early morning night. Only the room tone.

~Fin~

Acknowledgements

Heartfelt thanks —

To the film-makers of the world, too numerous to list, who have informed my work, my dreams, and my travel since childhood. Thanks also to those with whom I have worked in film, in Canada, the US, the UK, France, Italy, and Greece.

To my heart-brother, the late Jay Scott: Seeing fine films is a splendid thing — but it was always better with you.

To the Toronto International Film Festival for always introducing me to artists whose work I then can continue to seek and see.

To the hair and makeup people, to whom one trustingly gives one's face in the early morning (and is always better for it … unless supposed to be worse).

To the film crews, who always have the best and most honest information.

To sound directors, who, when I was 13, introduced me to the meditation that is "Room Tone."

To Lisette LeFevre, "Drobe" extraordinaire.

To the small invisible scene bird that sometimes lives inside your eyes where the camera can find it and lift you both way high in the sky while you do not appear to be moving.

To the Shoebridgians with whom I worked at SIFT, Ottawa 1990-1994, particularly Kate, Denis, Phil and Micheline and the participants who grew to be friends.

To my literary representative, Peter William Taylor, who is a passionate advocate for my books and incipient books.

To Pirkko Lindberg, Timo Lappalainen and colleagues for showing me Helsinki/Helsingfors.

To Bo and Ishrat Lindblad, Håkan Bravinger, Heidi von Born, and Francoise Sule for great generosity to me in Stockholm.

To Maria Zennström, Linda Boström, and Tor Eystein Øverås for their knowledge of and passion for cinema.

And to the quattri of Quattro Books, Beatriz, Luciano, John, and Allan. You have honoured me by asking me to be your first "Novellana." I salute you all, particularly literary editor for *Room Tone*, John Calabro, and copy-editor, Allan Briesmaster.

We are embarked — *avanti tutti e tutte!*

Gale Zoë Garnett

Toronto, Canada
December, 2006